William W. Osgoodby

Phonetic Shorthand

A complete manual of Pitman's phonography with all the modern

improvements

William W. Osgoodby

Phonetic Shorthand
A complete manual of Pitman's phonography with all the modern improvements

ISBN/EAN: 9783337399801

Printed in Europe, USA, Canada, Australia, Japan

Cover: Foto ©Andreas Hilbeck / pixelio.de

More available books at **www.hansebooks.com**

PHONETIC SHORTHAND.

A COMPLETE MANUAL OF PITMAN'S PHONOGRAPHY
WITH ALL THE MODERN IMPROVEMENTS.

BY WILLIAM W. OSGOODBY,

THIRTY-FOUR YEARS OFFICIAL STENOGRAPHER OF THE NEW YORK SUPREME COURT; EX-PRESIDENT OF THE
NEW YORK STATE STENOGRAPHER'S ASSOCIATION; FOREIGN ASSOCIATE OF THE LONDON
SHORTHAND SOCIETY; AUTHOR OF THE PHONETIC SHORTHAND
WORD-BOOK, SPEED-BOOK, ETC.

EIGHTH EDITION.

ROCHESTER, N. Y.
WILLIAMS & ROGERS.
1896

To ISAAC PITMAN,

By whose Genius the Basis of Phonographic Art was laid, and to the many Practitioners by whose Labors it has been brought to its present State of Perfection, all Stenographers of the English-speaking World owe a Debt of profound Gratitude.

ALPHABET.

CONSONANTS.			DUPLICATES.		
NAME.		**SOUND.**	**NAME.**		**SOUND.**
Pe	\	P in PIP	Iss	`. o`	S in BLISS
			Ses	`o`	Ses in BASES
Be	\	B in BIB	Ist	`o`	St in BLAST
Te	|	T in TIGHT	Ster	`0`	Ster in ULSTER
De	|	D in DIED	Ye	`u n`	Y in YOKE
			We	`c ɔ`	W in WALK
Chay	/	CH in ETCH			
Jay	/	J in EDGE	**LONG VOWELS.**		
Kay	—	K in KICK	Ē	`.|`	as in BEAT
Gay	—	G in GIG	Ā	`.|`	as in BAIT
Ef	\	F in FIFE	AH	`.|`	as in BALM
Ve	\	V in VIVE	AW	`⁻|`	as in BOUGHT
Ith	(	TH in THIN	Ō	`⁻|`	as in BOAT
The	(	TH in THEN	ŌŌ	`_|`	as in BOOT
Es	)	S in HISS	**SHORT VOWELS.**		
Ze	)	Z in HIS	Ĭ	`.|`	as in BIT
Ish	⌣	SH in ASSURE	Ĕ	`.|`	as in BET
Zhe	⌣	ZH in AZURE	Ă	`.|`	as in BAT
Lay	⌐	L in LEAL	Ŏ	`⁻|`	as in BOG
Ar	⌐	R in ROAR	Ŭ	`⁻|`	as in BUN
Ray	⁄	R in ROAR	ŎŎ	`_|`	as in FOOT
Em	⌢	M in MAIM	**DIPHTHONGS.**		
En	⌣	N in NUN			
Yay	⌐	Y in YEA	Ī	`v|`	as in BITE
Way	⌐	W in WAY	OI	`^|`	as in BOIL
Hay	⌢	H in HAY	OW	`^|`	as in BOUT
Ing	⌣	NG in SONG	EW	`^|`	as in BREW

PHONETIC SHORTHAND.

Sec. 1. Introductory.—a. In Phonetic Shorthand words are spelled as they are pronounced, and no silent letters are used. In the English alphabet the sounds of Ch as in *chain*, Th in *thin*, Sh in *show*, and Ng in *sing*, are not provided with distinct letters, though they are really simple sounds. The same letter often indicates different sounds, in different words, as the letter G, in the words *gun, gem;* the use of two or more letters to indicate a sound for which a single character is provided, is also very frequent, as the sound of F in the word *trough, triumph;* and a single, simple sound is often indicated by letters to which entirely different values are usually assigned, as in the words *pleasure, azure,* the letters S and Z are used to indicate a sound which has no precise representative in the language. Similar inconsistencies exist with respect to vowel sounds. In Phonetic Shorthand, however, each distinct vocal sound is provided with a distinct letter.

b. The alphabet should be carefully studied, and the *names* of the letters should be learned in connection with their sounds. The letters Chay and Gay, for instance, which represent the sound of Ch and the "hard" sound of G, should not be called *see-aitch* and *jee.* There is probably no better way to commit the letters to memory, than to trace them repeatedly with a penholder, pointed like a pencil, the sound of each letter being pronounced aloud as it is traced ; varying the exercise by frequently writing the letters with particular attention to form and to the proper angle with the line of writing.

c. It is only by careful and persistent practice, not only in writing but in reading his shorthand notes, that a legible style can be acquired by the student ; and an illegible style is worthless, even though written at high rate of speed. Every character should be made with precision, and no attempt should be

1

made to write rapidly; speed will come when practice has given the necessary facility for smooth and graceful writing.

d. The different principles should be taken in order, and each thoroughly understood before the next one is taken up. These principles do not apply to single words alone—they apply to *classes* of words and phrases; and if any one of them be misunderstood or misapplied, the error is far-reaching, involving all the words or phrases in the language to which the rule is applicable.

e. The student should not be satisfied with once reading the engraved exercises; they should be read and copied in shorthand many times, until each word-form can be recognized instantly. The same care should be taken in the use of the writing exercises, which begin on page 73. The value of one's knowledge in this study, depends not only upon his perfect familiarity with every principle, but upon his ability to apply each of those principles readily and correctly; and this ability can only be attained by earnest and painstaking effort.

f. The proper use of punctuation will very much aid the student in reading his written exercises. The following marks are used in shorthand: ✕ Period; ⁄⁄ Semicolon; ⚊ Hyphen; ∿∿ Dash; ⫶⫶ Interrogation; ⚡ Exclamation; / Paragraph. Excepting these, the ordinary marks of punctuation are used. The dot of the comma should be distinctly made. "*Stet.*" written in the margin of the notes, indicates that an erasure has been made by mistake. Particular emphasis to a word or phrase is indicated by underscoring it with a waved line. If more than one outline is to be underscored, a light, straight line is used. Two inclined ticks are placed under a word to indicate that it should be written with a capital in transcribing notes; as,

When   Envy   cannot deny   Merit,   it ignores it.

A proper name, consisting of two or more words may be underscored with a light, straight line; as, /ˋ ⚊ ⟍ₓ

THE ALPHABET.

Sec. 2. The alphabet of Phonetic Shorthand contains forty letters, representing the forty elementary sounds of the English language. These letters are divided into two general classes, namely, Consonants and Vowels. The consonant sounds are represented by straight and curved lines (called *stems*), and the vowels by dots, dashes, and angles. The stems of a word are written together, each stem after the first one being joined to the one preceding it, without lifting the pen; and the stems thus joined are termed the *outline* of the word. The vowels are inserted after the outline is thus completed.

a. The names of the letters, and the sounds indicated by them, must be thoroughly learned. Make the stems uniform in length, and exact in form, direction, and shading. Write on ruled paper—paper ruled with double lines is by far the best—and always write with pen and ink. When stems are joined at an angle, make the angle distinct. When two straight stems are joined without an angle, write them with a continuous straight line twice the length of a single stem; and if one stem be light and the other heavy, shade them carefully into each other. (*See illustrations on page 5.*)

b. In writing the exercises upon the consonants, the first upright or inclined stem in an outline should be placed upon the line; and if the first stem be horizontal, followed by a stem struck upward or downward, the former must be placed in such position that the latter may rest upon the line; but if all the stems of an outline be horizontal, it should be written on the line.

CONSONANTS.

Sec. 3. The consonants are divided into three groups, viz. : 1. Regular Straight Stems; 2. Regular Curved Stems; 3. Irregular Stems. The regular stems are arranged in pairs, the second one of each pair being shaded, thus indicating the natural distinction between the vocal and whispered sounds represented by them. The irregular stems are not thus paired.

Note.—The sound of Th in *them*, is indicated by the letters Dh, in the rules and writing exercises, the name of the stem being pronounced like the word *the*.

a. Regular Straight Stems.—These are all written downward, except Kay and Gay, which are written from left to right. Great care should be taken to strike these stems in the exact directions shown in the engraving. (*See lines 1 and 2.*)

WRITING EXERCISE.

P, b, t, d, ch, j, k, g; p-b t-d, ch-j, k-g, p-t, t-p, b-t, t-b, t-k, k-t, t-ch, ch-t, k-p, p-k, k-b, b-k, k-ch, ch-k, ch-g, g-ch, k-j, j-k, d-t, b-p, g-k, p-p, t-t, k-k, b-b, d-d, g-g, j-j, k-d, d-k, p-ch, ch-p, b-ch, ch-b, b-j, j-b, t-b-k, k-b-t.

b. Regular Curved Stems.—These may all be written downward, at present. Rules will hereafter be given for writing Sh upward in certain cases. Shade the heavy curves carefully, to give them a graceful appearance. Light and heavy curves are shaded into each other, when joined without an angle. (*Lines 3–5.*)

WRITING EXERCISE.

F, v, th, dh (*the*), s, z, sh, zh; f-g, g-f, f-p, p-f, s-p, t-th, ch-s, f-th, sh-f, v-g, g-th, g-dh, f-b, b-f, s-b, t-dh, ch-z, f-dh, sh-v, k-f, s-k, f-t, f-v, s-t, d-dh, j-s, f-v, sh-z, v-f, k-sh, f-ch, p-th, sh-p, t-s, p-sh, f-sh, s-s, g-v, g-sh, f-j, b-th, sh-b, t-z, b-sh. f-th, s-z, k-th, sh-k, th-t, p-dh, sh-d, d-s, ch-sh, d-z, j-sh, v-sh, s-v, f-f, th-th, s-s, sh-sh, v-v, dh-dh.

c. Irregular Stems.—L is written upward, when standing alone, and in most other cases. Rules will hereafter be given for striking it downward under some circumstances. Ar, Way, and Yay are struck downward. M, N, Ing, and Hay are struck from left to right. Ray, which is a duplicate for R, is always struck upward, and is more inclined than Chay. (*Lines 6–14.*)

WRITING EXERCISE.

L-p, p-l, l-t, t-l, l-ch, ch-l, l-k, k-l, l-b, b-l, l-d, d-l, l-j, j-l, l-g, g-l, l-f, f-l, l-v, v-l, l-th, th-l, l-s, s-l, l-z, z-l. P-m, m-b, t-m, m-d, ch-m, m-j, k-m, m-k, g-m, m-g, m-n, n-m, m-l, l-m, n-l, l-n, l-ng. (*Use Ar.*) P-r, r-p, t-r, d-r, ch-r, r-m, l-r, r-l, r-sh, sh-r. W-k, w-l, w-r. Y-l, y-k. (*Use Ray, for Italic letters.*) R-ch, ch-r, r-r, r-p, ch-p, r-k, k-r, p-r, p-ch, p-r, r-d, ch-d, b-r, b-ch, f-r, f-ch, f-r, m-r, m-ch, n-r, n-ch, r-n, ch-n, r-sh, sh-r, r-z, z-r, z-r.

REGULAR STRAIGHT STEMS.

Pee \ Bee \ Tee Dee | Chay / Jay / Kay __ Gay __

1

2

REGULAR CURVED STEMS.

Ef Vee Ith Dhe (Es Zee) Ish Zhe

3

4

5

IRREGULAR STEMS.

Lay Ar Em En Ing Yay Way Hay Ray

6

7

8

9

10

11

12

13

14

VOWELS.

Sec. 4. There are sixteen vowel sounds provided for in Phonetic Shorthand, and these are divided into three classes, namely: 1. Long Vowels; 2. Short Vowels; 3. Diphthongs. Long vowels are indicated by a heavy dot or dash, placed at the beginning, middle, or end of a consonant stem; short vowels, by a light dot or dash similarly placed; diphthongs, by compound characters, placed at the beginning or end of a stem. The vowel signs are called first-, second-, or third-place, according to the positions they thus occupy. If placed at the left of any upright or inclined stem, or above a horizontal stem, a vowel sign is read before the stem; if placed at the right of an upright or inclined stem, or below a horizontal stem, it is read after the stem. When vowels are inserted in an outline, it is said to be *vocalized*. *

a. Long Vowels.—These are indicated by heavy dots or dashes, placed near the stem, in the positions above described. Dash vowels are struck at right angles with the stem, but must not be allowed to touch it. The sound of â, as in *fair, dare*, is indicated by the second-place heavy dot. (*See lines 1–3.*)

b. Positions of Words.—Few vowels are used by reporters, but the leading or accented vowel is indicated by the position in which the outline is written.

1. When the accented vowel is a first-place vowel, the *first upright or inclined stem* of the outline is written above the line. (*Lines 4–6.*)

2. When the accented vowel is second-place, such stem is written on the line. (*Lines 7–9.*)

3. When the accented vowel is third-place, such stem is written through the line. (*Lines 10–12.*)

If the outline contain horizontal stems only, it is written above the line, on the line, or below the line, in like accordance with the position of its accented vowel. (*Lines 13–14.*)

---

* Writing exercises under this section, will be found on page 73, *post.*

6

LONG VOWELS.

ĒĒ	Ā	AH	AW	Ō	ŌŌ

c. Short Vowels.—These are indicated by light dots and dashes. The difference in the sizes of the long and short vowels should be distinct, but without making the former so heavy as to detract from the beauty of the writing. The sound of ẽ, as in *mercy*, is indicated by the second-place light dot. (*Lines 1-5.*)

d. Vowels between Consonants.—When a vowel occurs between two stems, observe the following rules :

1. First-place vowels are written after the first stem.

2. Second-place long vowels (ā, ō) are written after the first stem.

3. Second-place short vowels (ĕ, ŭ) are written before the second stem.

4. Third-place vowels are written before the second stem.

Notice carefully the illustrations of each of these rules, in lines 1 to 8. See, also, Diagram of Vowels, p. 71.

e. Diphthongs.—These signs should be accurately made, and should never be inclined from the perpendicular. The character for I, in words containing more than one stem, may be written in either the first or third place, but it is always to be considered as first-place when the position of an outline depends upon it. (*Lines 9-12.*)

f. A small tick, joined to one of these signs, indicates that another vowel sound follows the diphthong. (*Line 13.*)

g. When two vowels occur between two stems, one of them may be written to each ; or both vowels may be indicated by an acute angle, inclined in the direction of Chay, written in the place of the first of the two vowels. This angle opens upward if the first one be a dot vowel, and downward if it be a dash vowel. The down-stroke of the angle is shaded, if the first vowel to be indicated be long. (*Line 14.*)

h. When two vowels are written to the same stem, the one pronounced nearest the stem is placed somewhat nearer it than the other. (*Line 15.*)

i. When a word begins with I or Oi, the diphthong sign may often be joined to the stem. The signs for I, Ow, and Ew, may sometimes be joined to a stem at the end of a word. (*Line 15.*)

SHORT VOWELS.

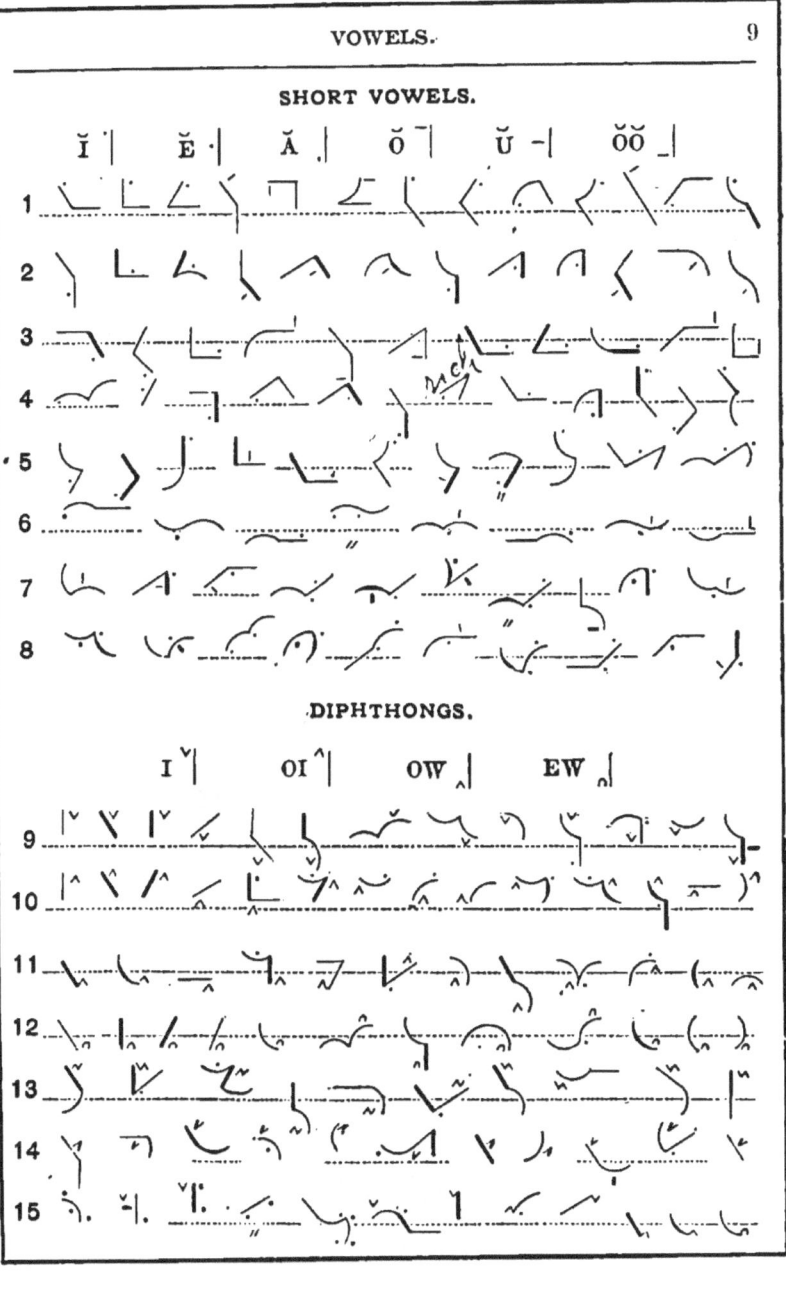

DIPHTHONGS.

j. W and Y are often conveniently indicated by small semi-circles prefixed to a stem. The semi-circle for W may open either to the right or left; that for Y, either upward or downward. They should be written in such direction as to make a distinct angle with the stem, and vowels may be placed to the stem in the same manner as if the semi-circle were not used. (*Lines 1, 2.*)

RULES FOR WRITING L, R, AND SH.

Sec. 5. When the stems representing L, R, and Sh, are written upward, they are named Lay, Ray and Shay, respectively; when written downward, they are named El, Ar, and Ish. The following rules are to be observed, in forming outlines containing these stems:

a. When L is the only consonant stem in a word, Lay is used. (*Line 3.*)

b. When L is the first consonant in an outline containing other stems, El is used if preceded by a vowel; and Lay, if not. (*Line 4.*)

c. When L is the last consonant represented by a stem, in an outline containing other stems, Lay is used if followed by a vowel; and El, if not. (*Line 5.*)

d. When R is the first or only stem in a word, Ar is used if a vowel precede it; and Ray, if not. (*Line 6.*)

e. When R is the last consonant represented by a stem, in an outline containing other stems, Ray is used if followed by a vowel; and Ar, if not. (*Line 7.*)

f. When Sh begins an outline, or when it is the only consonant stem in a word, Ish is used. (*Line 8.*)

g. When Sh is the last consonant, in an outline containing other stems, Shay is used if followed by a vowel; and Ish, if not. (*Line 9.*)

Make the following exceptions to the foregoing rules:

h. Lay is used before P, B, T, D, F, V, Th, Dh, Sh, Zh, Lay, Y, and Ray; and after S, Z, Sh, Zh, Lay, R, M, W, and Y. El is usually employed after N and Ng. (*Lines 10, 11.*)

i. Ray is used before T, D, Ch, J, Th, Dh, F, and V; and after Th, Dh, M, and H. Ar is used before M and H. (*Line 12.*)

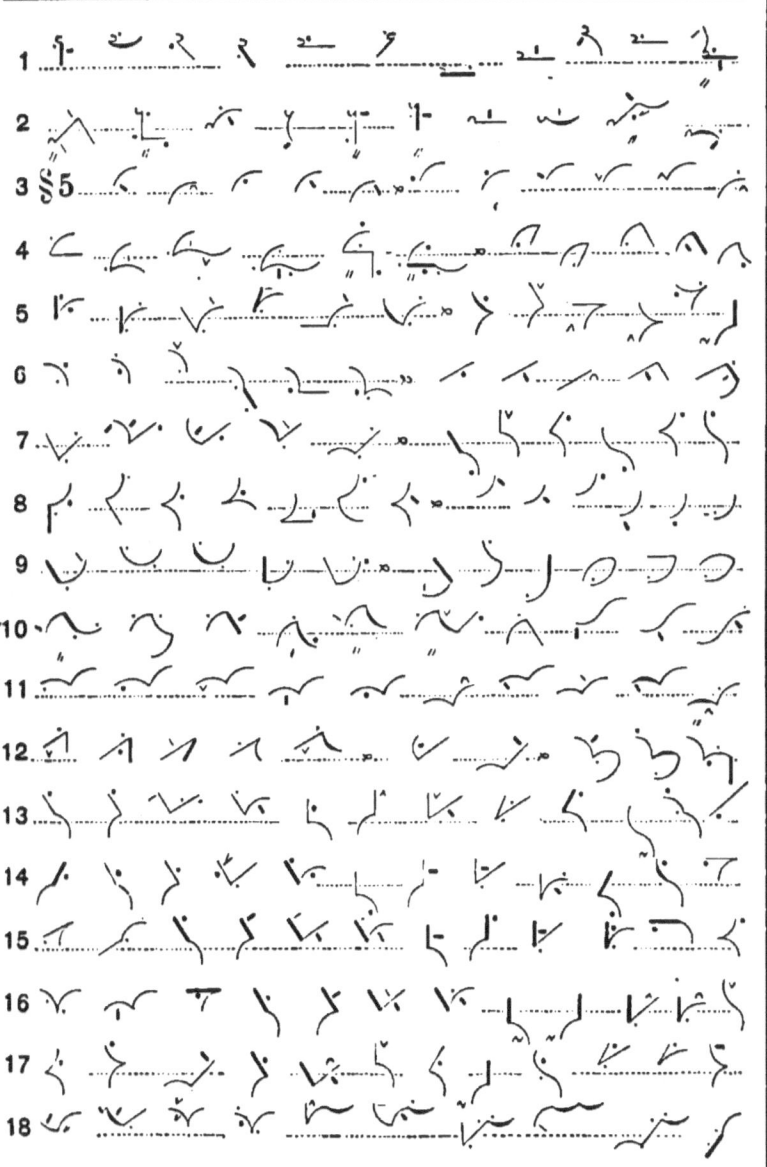

THE ASPIRATE.

Sec. 6. The stem ⌒ is seldom used, but the sound of H is usually indicated in one of the following ways: 1. By a small dot opposite a vowel sign; 2. By a light tick ⁄ struck in the direction of Chay, whenever it will make an acute angle with the succeeding stem; 3. By writing a dash vowel parallel with the stem. (*Lines 1-3.*)

a. For the sound of Wh (pronounced *hw*), the tick may be shaded, or it may be prefixed to the stem or semicircle W. (*Line 4.*)

WORD-SIGNS AND CONTRACTIONS.

Sec. 7. Abbreviated forms, called *word-signs* and *contractions*, are used for words of very frequent occurrence. A word-sign may be either a vowel sign, a circle, or a loop, or a simple stem. A contraction is formed of more than one stem, or of a single stem having some attachment (as a circle, or hook), the whole sign indicating some prominent portion of the word represented by it. These abbreviated forms are written in various positions, generally dependent upon the position of the accented vowel of the word. In some instances, two or more words are represented by the same sign, but when written in a sentence the context will invariably determine which word is intended. (*Lines 5-12.*)

☞ *Write Exercises I., II., and III., of the Speed-Book.*

a. Phrasing.—Two or more word-signs, if closely related in sense, may be joined in a phrase-sign. The first stem of the phrase is generally written in its usual position, the others following it without lifting the pen. (*Line 12.*)

KEY TO LINE 12.—Before-that. It-was. Shall-come. They-do. Do-they. Which-can. Or-that. Which-was. Can-do. That-was. Was-that. It-was-no.

b. Small ticks, one-fourth the length of a stem, are used for certain words, and they are named, from the stems they resemble, the *P-tick, T-tick, Chay-tick, Ray-tick*, etc.

I.—Use the P- or Ray-tick for *I*, before any stem except Ar and Way; and before those stems use the T-tick only. In the

12

1 §6

2

3

4

WORD-SIGNS.

The ... A . An,And . All ... Too,Two . Who , I,High ... On ... He ...
Put ... Before \ What,Ought ... At,It,Take | Out,To,Took ...
Did ! Do | Had ... Watch.Each ... Which.Change / Come,Came ...
Can ... Give-n ... If ... For ... Of,Live ... Have ... With ...
They (That (... Was) As,Has) ... She,Wish ... Shall)
Should) ... Will,Well (Hear,Here,From ... Were) Our,Hour ...
Or ... Their,There ... In,Any ... You-r ... We,Why ...
Away, Would ... Him ... When ... How ...

5

6

7

8

9

10

11

12

middle, or at the end of a phrase-sign, *I* is always indicated by the T-tick. (*See lines 1-3.*)

HE.—Use the Chay-tick only, for *He*, at the beginning of a phrase. In other places, use any inclined tick that will make a sharp angle with the stem. (*See lines 4, 5.*)

THE.—Use the Chay- or Ray-tick for *The*, before or after another word; except that the P-tick may be used after a stem wherever it will make a better angle. (*See lines 6-9.*)

A, AN, AND.—Use the Kay-tick for these words, wherever it will make a distinct angle. In other cases, use the T-tick. (*See lines 10, 11.*)

Write *and a, and an* ⌐ , *and the, and he* ⇁ , on a ⌐ , on the ⌐ .

☞ See further explanations of the ticks, page 77, *post.*

c.   Where two different ticks are provided for either of the above words, that one should be used which will make the most distinct angle with the word-sign to which it is attached, and a tick cannot be used where it will not make a distinct angle.

SMALL CIRCLE FOR S AND Z.

Sec. 8.   S is most frequently represented by a small circle, initial or final, named Iss, written on the right side of an upright or inclined straight stem (except Ray), on the upper side of Ray, Kay, and Gay; and on the inner side of curved stems. The sound of Z may also be represented by the small final circle.

a.   Between two straight stems which form an angle, a circle is written outside the angle. If one or both stems be curved, the circle is written within the curve. (*Lines 12, 13.*)

b.   An initial circle is always read before the stem, and before any vowels written to the stem. A final circle is always read after the stem, and after all vowels written to the stem. When the tick for H, or for Wh, is written before an initial circle, a vowel sound is always to be understood as occurring between the tick and the circle. The particular vowel will be sufficiently indicated, if the outline is written in its proper position. (*Lines 13-18.*)

☞ *Write Exercise IV. of the Speed-Book.*

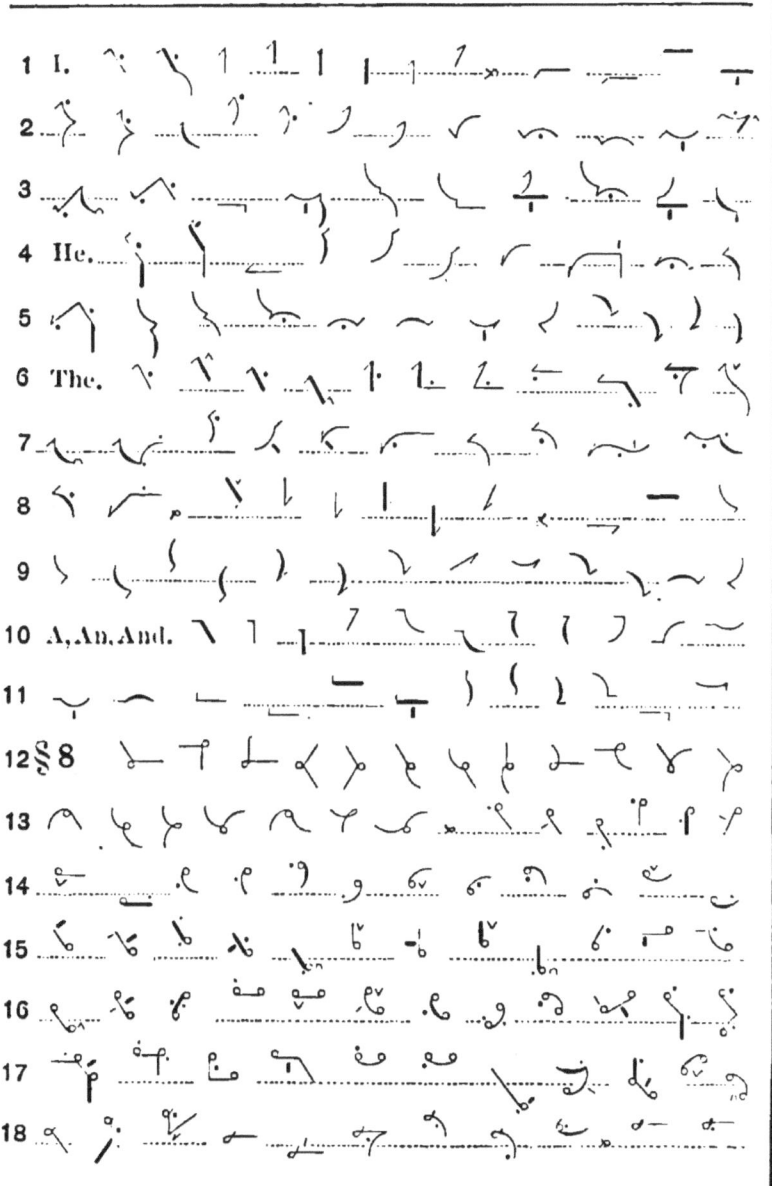

c. When a vowel precedes S or Z, at the beginning of a word, and when a word ends with S or Z followed by a vowel, the stem must be used. The stem must also be used when S or Z is the only consonant in a word, and when two vowels occur between S or Z and a preceding or succeeding stem. (*Lines 1-3.*)

d. When a singular noun ends with a stem S or Z, the circle is added to form the plural number or the possessive case ; also, to form the third person, singular, of a regular verb ending with either of these stems. (*Compare Sec. 9, a.*) The circle may also be added to a word sign, for the same purpose. (*Line 4.*)

e. If a circle occurs between two stems, vowels are necessarily written to the stem with which they are pronounced. (*Lines 5, 6.*)

f. When Z is the first consonant in a word, the stem must be used. (*Line 7.*)

g. A small hook may be made on the back of a stem ending with a circle, to indicate the sound of N following that of S ; and another circle may be written within the hook for a final S. (*Lines 8, 9.*)

h. The circle is sometimes used for Sh, and with the back-hook forms the termination Tion, as is more fully explained in section 22.

i. If R is the only stem in a word, and it is preceded and followed by vowels, and also preceded by a circle or loop, Ray is used. Ray is also used when R is preceded by a circle or loop and followed by a downward stem. (*See Sec. 10.*) (*Line 10.*)

j. Phrasing.—*Is, His, As, Has, Us,* or *Say,* is added to another word by the small circle. (*Line 11.*)

k. *Is, His, As,* or *Has,* is prefixed to another word by the small circle. When thus used, *Is* and *His* are always written above the line, and *As* and *Has* on the line. (*Line 12.*)

KEY TO LINES 11 AND 12.—All-is. Who-is. He-is. He-has. Before-his. What-is. Had-his. Which-has. For-us. Above-us. With-us. From-his. There-is.

Is-he. Has-he. As-if. As-though. As-was. As-shall. As-will. As-you. As-we. Is-so. Is-without. His-own.

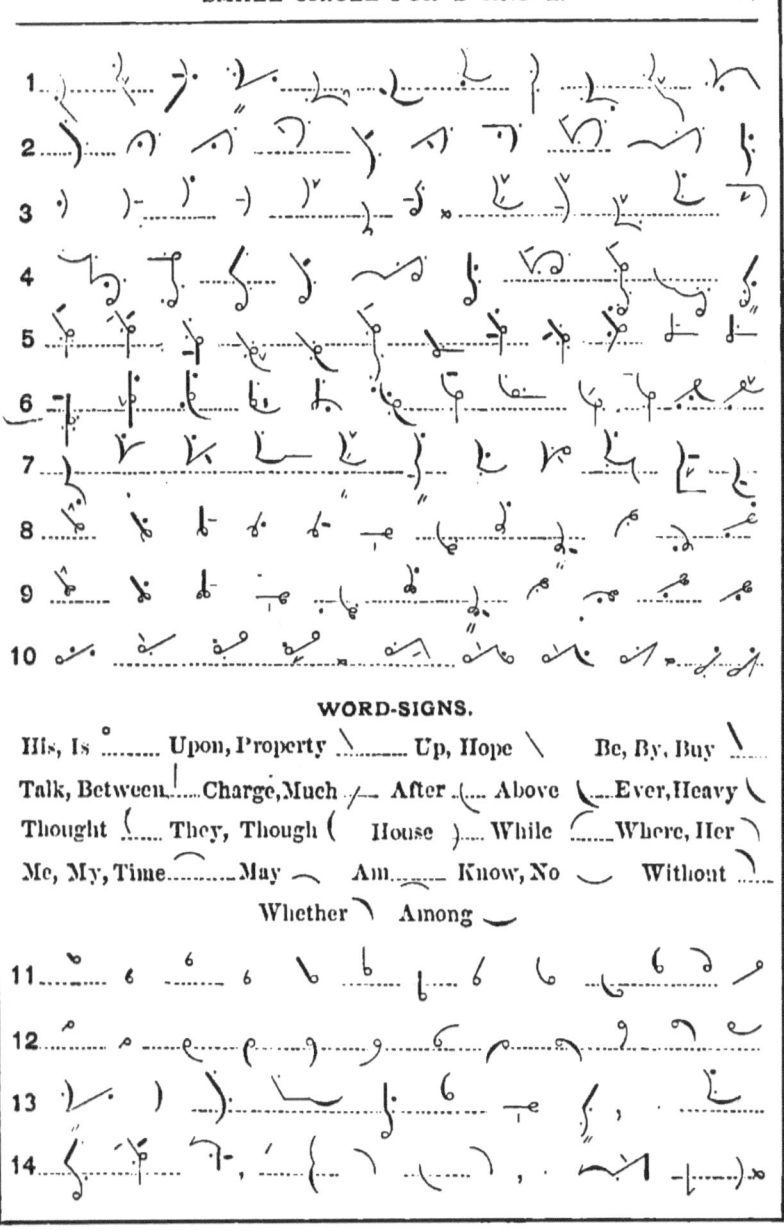

WORD-SIGNS.

His, Is .... Upon, Property .... Up, Hope \   Be, By, Buy \

Talk, Between...... Charge, Much .... After ...... Above ......Ever, Heavy \

Thought .... They, Though (House)..... While ......Where, Her)

Me, My, Time........... May ⌒   Am...... Know, No ⌣   Without)

Whether) Among ⌣

LARGE CIRCLE FOR SES AND SEZ.

Sec. 9. A large circle, called Ses, indicates that syllable or any similar one. It is written on the same side of a stem as the Iss-circle. It may be vocalized by writing a vowel sign within it, and, if desired, the exact vowel may be indicated by placing the sign in the upper, middle, or lower part of the circle. (*Line 1.*)

a. The plural number, or the possessive case of a noun ending with Iss, is indicated by enlarging the circle. The third person, singular, of a regular verb ending with Iss, is indicated in the same manner. (*Compare Sec. 8, d.*) (*Line 2.*)

b. A small circle may be written within a final large circle, for the additional sound of S. (*Line 3.*)

c. Phrasing.—*Is his, As has,* and similar phrases, are prefixed or added to a word-sign by the large circle, *Is his* being written above the line, and *As has* on the line, when used initially. *Is* or *As* is prefixed to an initial Iss-circle, or added to a final one, by enlarging the circle. (*Line 4.*)

KEY TO LINE 4. It-is-his. What-is-his. Which-is-his. Before-his-is. If-his-is. For-as-is. It-is-as-large. Is-said. Is-supposed. Is-such. As-such

☞ *Write Exercise V. of the Speed-Book.*

LOOPS FOR ST AND STR.

Sec. 10. Iss is changed into a short loop, to indicate the sound of St ; and by widening and lengthening the loop, Str is indicated. The Str-loop is not used initially.

a. The St-loop is less than half the length of a stem ; the Str-loop extends to the middle of a stem. (*Lines 5-10.*)

b. A final circle is added to either loop for S. A hook on the back of a stem, after a loop, indicates N or Ng, and a final Iss-circle may be written within the back-hook. (*Lines 11, 12.*)

c. An initial loop is read before the stem, and before any vowel written to the stem. A final loop is read after the stem, and after all vowels written to the stem.

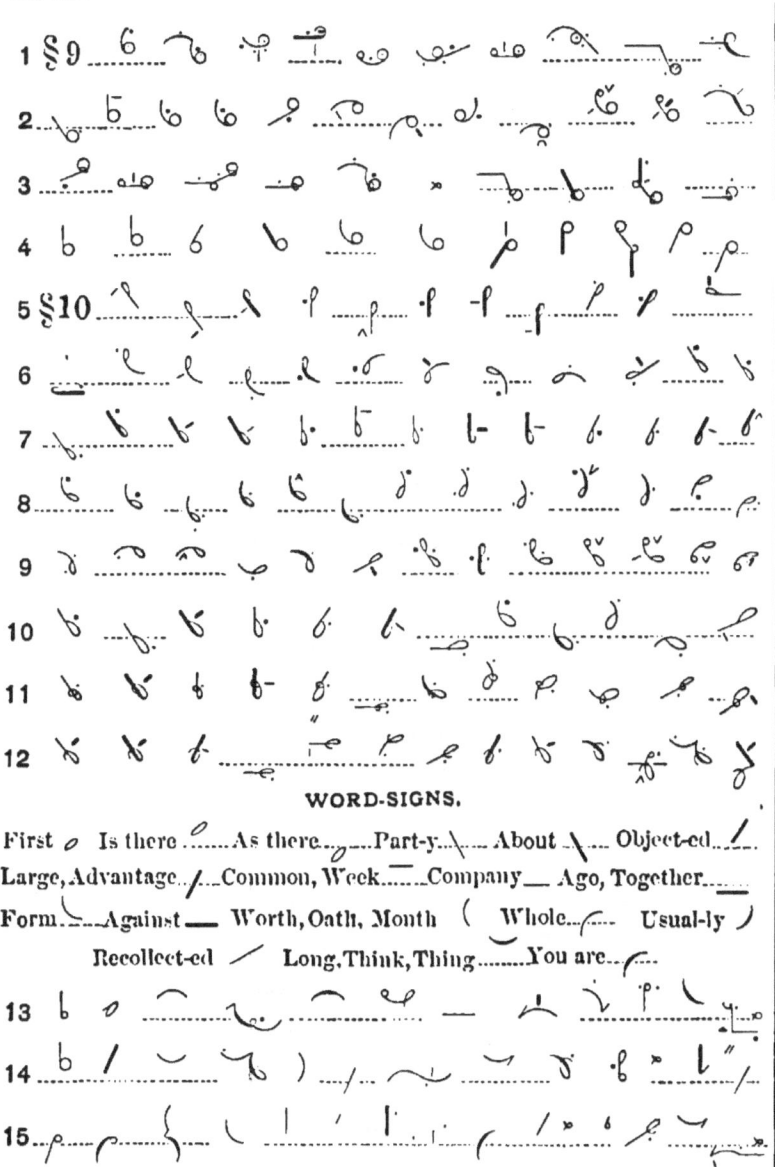

WORD-SIGNS.

First *o* Is there *o* As there *,,* Part-y ** About ** Object-ed */*

Large, Advantage */* Common, Week *—* Company *—* Ago, Together *—*

Form *⌐* Against *—* Worth, Oath, Month *(* Whole *⌐* Usual-ly *)*

Recollect-ed */* Long, Think, Thing *—* You are *⌐*

d. A final circle or loop may be shaded, to distinguish Z from S. (*Line 1.*)

e. Phrasing.—The small loop adds to a word-sign the words *Is it, Is the, As it, As the, Has it, Has the,* or *First.* The verb *State* may also be prefixed or added to a word-sign by this loop. When a word ends with the Iss-circle, the word *It* or *The* may be added, by changing the circle to a loop. In the same manner, the word *Their* or *There* may be indicated by the use of the large loop. (*Line 2.*)

KEY TO LINE 2.—What-is-it. What-is-there. It-is-the. It-is-there. Does-it. Does-their. Which-is-the. Which-is-their. At-first. State-what. State-whether. State-where. You-state.

☞ *Write Exercises VI. and VII. of the Speed-Book.*

COMBINATIONS OF CONSONANTS.

Sec. 11. Certain combinations of consonants are of frequent occurrence, and they are represented by attaching a hook to the stem indicating the first sound in such combinations. With respect to these hooks, the following rules must be carefully observed :

a. Initial hooks are read AFTER the stem to which they are attached, and AFTER all vowels written before the stem ; but BEFORE any vowels written after the stem, and BEFORE any final hook, circle, or loop.

b. Final hooks are read AFTER the stem to which they are attached, and AFTER all vowels or initial hooks, but BEFORE a final circle.

INITIAL HOOK FOR R.

Sec. 12. A small initial hook, on the LEFT side of any upright or inclined straight stem except Ray ; on the LOWER side of Ray. Kay, and Gay ; or on the inner side of a curved stem : indicates that the sound of R occurs immediately after the stem.

a. The consonants thus combined are named Per, Ber, etc., and vowels may be written before or after them in the same manner as to simple stems. (*Lines 3-11.*)

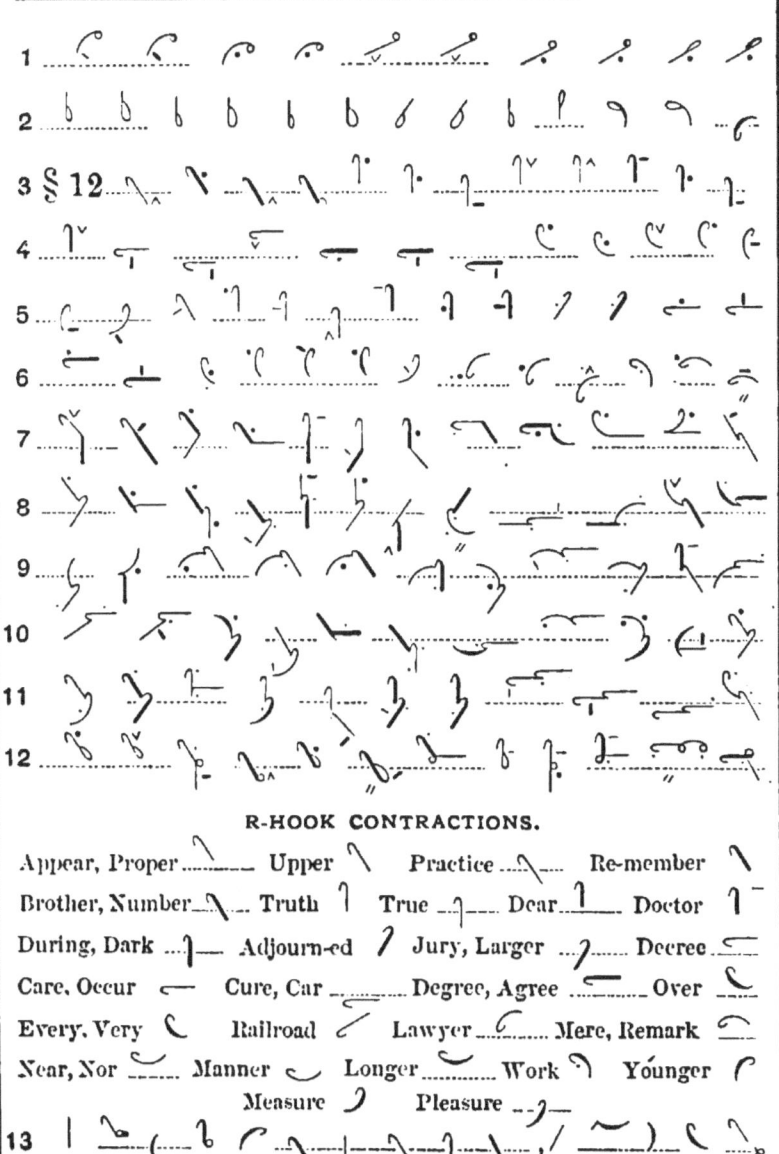

R-HOOK CONTRACTIONS.

Appear, Proper	Upper	Practice	Re-member
Brother, Number	Truth	True	Dear	Doctor
During, Dark	Adjourn-ed	Jury, Larger	Decree
Care, Occur	Cure, Car	Degree, Agree	Over
Every, Very	Railroad	Lawyer	Mere, Remark
Near, Nor	Manner	Longer	Work	Younger
	Measure	Pleasure	

b. When R is the last of two or more consonants in an outline, and is immediately preceded and followed by vowels, the stem must be used; also, when R is the last sound in a word and two vowels occur between it and a preceding stem; and generally when a long vowel precedes the sound of R. (*Lines 1-3.*)

c. Words ending with *-rer*, may be distinguished from those ending with *-rier*, by writing the former with Ar and the latter with Ray. (*Line 4.*)

d. Phrasing.—The R-hook adds to a word-sign the word *Or*, *Were*, or *Her*. (*Line 5.*)

KEY TO LINE 5.—Two-or-three. When-or-where. What-were-they. They-were. You-were. We-were. Where-were. Which-were. There-were. For-her With-her. When-her.

☞ *Write Exercise VIII. of the Speed-Book.*

INITIAL HOOK FOR L.

Sec. 13. A small initial hook, on the RIGHT side of any upright or inclined straight stem except Ray; or on the UPPER side of Ray, Kay, or Gay; indicates that the sound of L occurs immediately after the stem. (*Line 6.*)

a. A short, broad initial hook, on the inner side of curved stems, adds the sound of L in like manner. (*Line 7.*)

b. The consonants thus combined are named Pel, Bel, etc., and vowels are written before and after them in the same manner as to simple stems. (*Lines 6-9.*)

c. When L is the last of two or more consonants in an outline, and is immediately preceded and followed by vowels, the stem must be used; also, when L is the last sound in a word and two vowels occur between it and a preceding stem; and generally when a long vowel precedes the sound of L. (*Lines 10-12.*)

d. Words ending with *-rl* may be distinguished from those ending with *-ril*, *-rel*, *-rol*, etc., by writing the former with Ar and the latter with Ray. (*Line 13.*)

e. Phrasing.—The L-hook adds to a word-sign the word *All*, *Will*, or *Well*. (*Line 14.*)

KEY TO LINE 14.—Upon-all. About-all. At-all. For-all. Of-All. With-all. In-all. It-will. They-will. So-will. She-will. We-will. As-well.

☞ *Write Exercise IX. of the Speed-Book.*

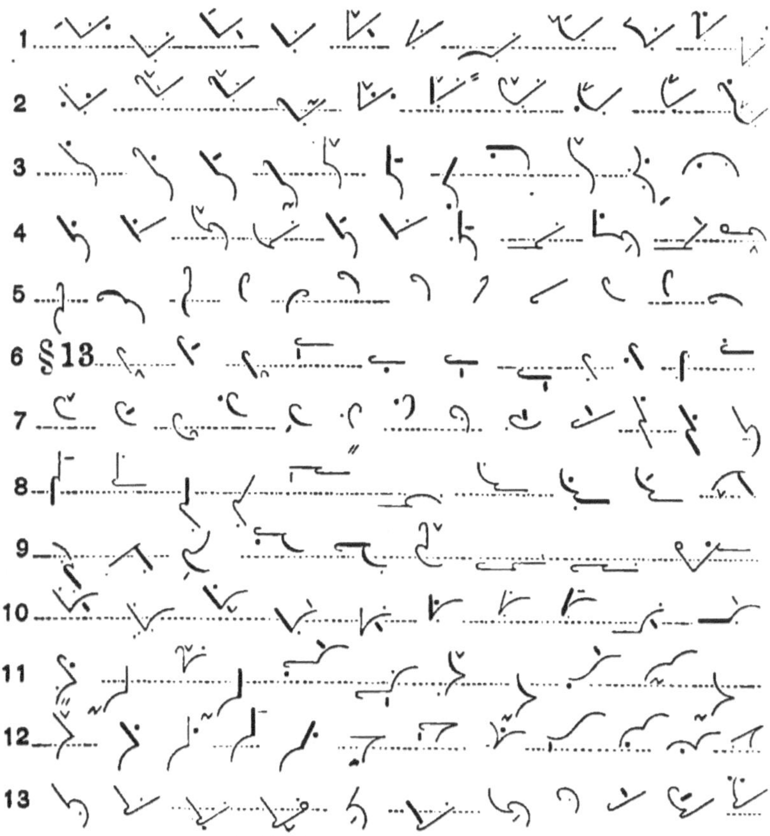

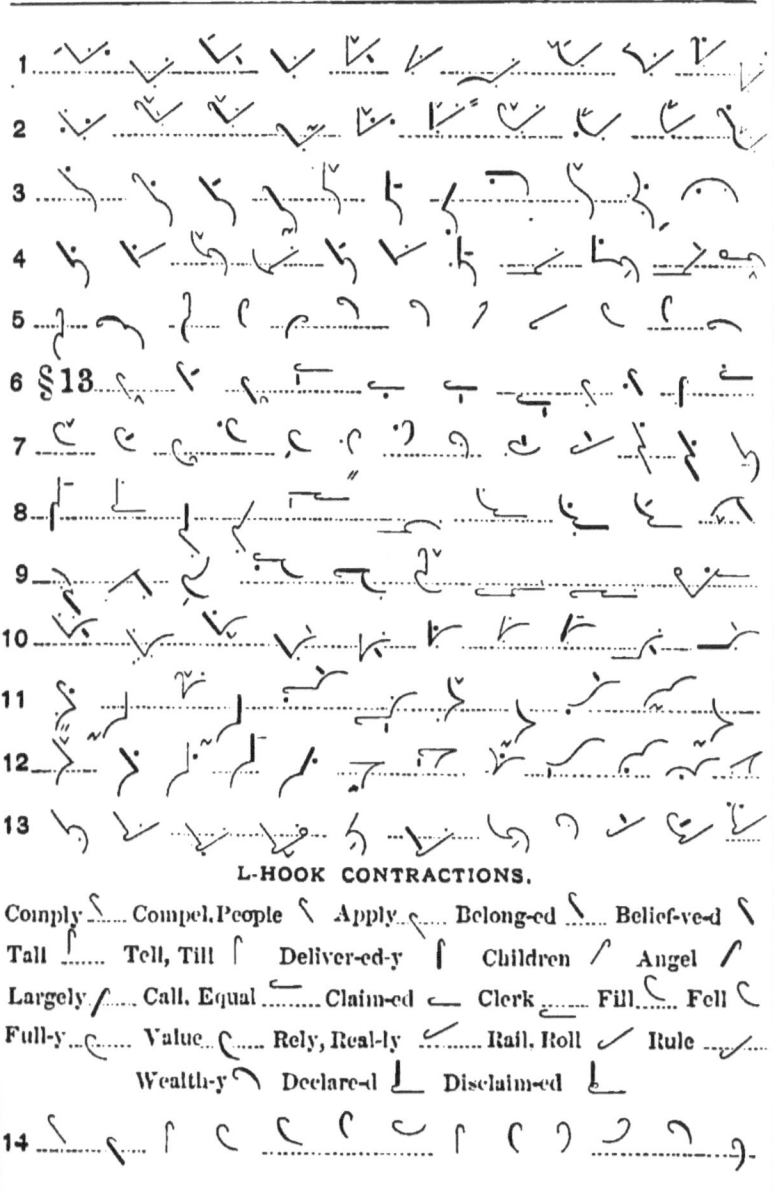

L-HOOK CONTRACTIONS.

Comply ..... Compel, People Apply ..... Belong-ed ..... Belief-ve-d
Tall ..... Tell, Till Deliver-ed-y Children Angel
Largely ..... Call, Equal ..... Claim-ed Clerk ..... Fill ..... Fell
Full-y ..... Value ..... Rely, Real-ly ..... Rail, Roll Rule .....
Wealth-y Declare-d Disclaim-ed

HOOKS COMBINED WITH CIRCLES AND LOOPS.

Sec. 14. Iss is combined with the R-hook, by changing the hook to a circle, on straight stems, and by writing the circle within the hook on curves. If the R-hook on a straight stem be changed to a loop, the sound of St is indicated as occurring before the stem and hook. (*Lines 1-3.*)

a. Iss is combined with the L-hook, on both straight and curved stems, by writing the circle within the hook. (*Line 4.*)

b. When combined with either the R-hook or the L-hook, the circle is read first; a vowel before the stem, next; the stem next; the hook next; and a vowel after the stem next.

c. Ses is never written within a hook or another circle.

d. When combinations of circles and hooks occur in the middle of a word, they are made as indicated in lines 5 to 7.

☞ *Write Exercise X. of the Speed-Book.*

VOCALIZATION OF INITIAL HOOKS.

Sec. 15. When vowels occur between stems and their initial hooks, they are indicated as follows: Dot vowels are represented by small circles, written in the position of the vowel, before the stem to indicate a long vowel, and after the stem to indicate a short vowel; and dash vowels and diphthongs are struck through or across the end of the hooked stem, in their proper positions. (*Lines 8-10.*)

☞ *Write Exercises XI. and XII. of the Speed-Book.*

FINAL HOOK FOR N.

Sec. 16. A small final hook, on the R-hook side of straight stems, and on the inner side of curves, indicates an added N.

a. The N-hook is always read after the stem to which it is attached, and after any vowel or initial hook written to the stem, but before a final circle. When N is the last consonant sound of a word and is followed by a vowel, the stem is used, and not the hook. (*Lines 11-14.*)

b. If two vowels occur between N and a preceding stem, the N-stem must be used, excepting such words as *criterion*, in which the hook is used. (*Line 15.*)

24

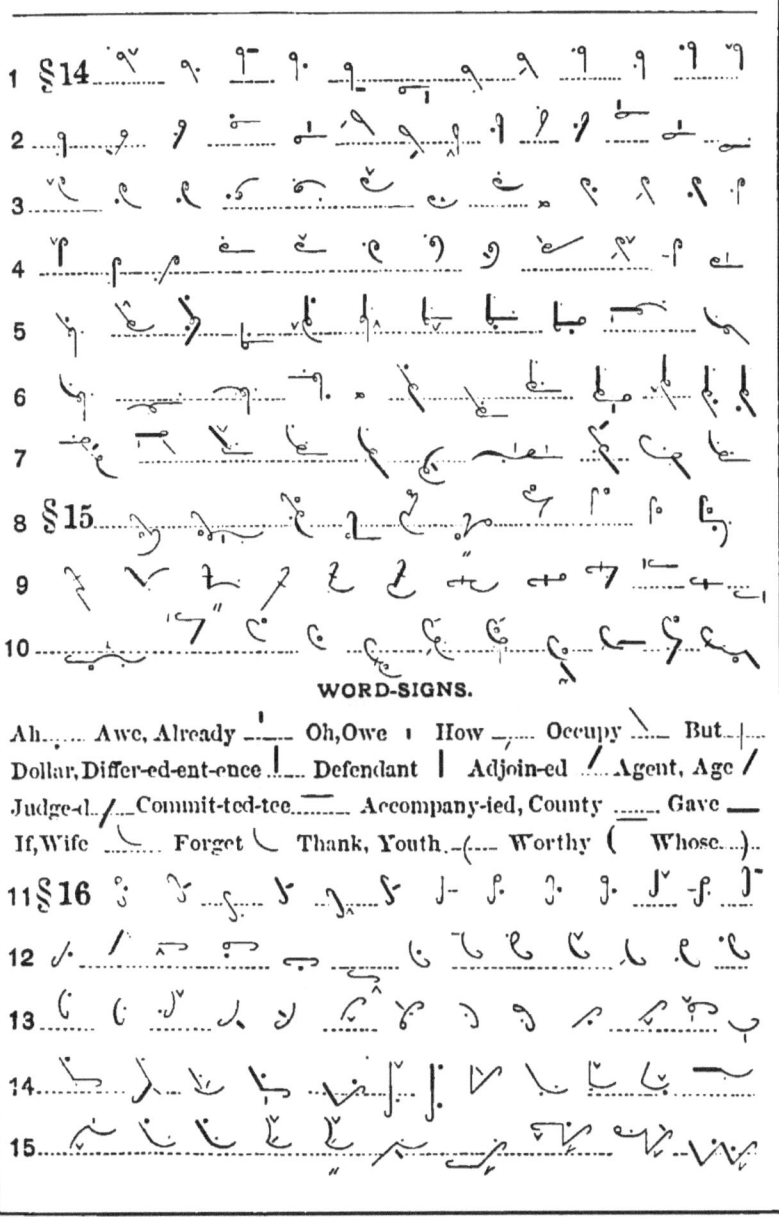

WORD-SIGNS.

Ah..... Awe, Already ..... Oh, Owe ı How .... Occupy ..... But.....
Dollar, Differ-ed-ent-ence ..... Defendant ı Adjoin-ed ..... Agent, Age /
Judge-d ..... Commit-ted-tee ..... Accompany-ied, County ..... Gave ....
If, Wife ..... Forget ⌣ Thank, Youth ...... Worthy (Whose...)..

c. The N-hook on a straight stem, when changed to a small circle, indicates Ns or Nz. If a back hook be added, it indicates Nsn, and a circle may be written within the back-hook for a final S. (*Lines 1-3.*)

d. The N-hook, on a straight stem, when changed to a loop, indicates Nst. If the loop be lengthened and widened, it indicates Nstr. A circle may be added to either loop, for a final S. (*Line 4.*)

e. The N-hook, on a straight stem, changed to a large circle, indicates N-ses or N-sez. (*Line 5.*)

f. S is added to the N-hook on curves, by writing the circle within the hook. (*Lines 6, 7.*)

g. Phrasing.—The N-hook adds to a word-sign the word *An, And, Not, Own,* or *Than.* (*Line 8.*)

KEY TO LINE 8.—About-an-hour. Half-an-hour. By-and-by. Off-and-on. You-and-I. Did-not-know. Cannot-be. Have-not-known. Our-own. Their-own. More-than.

N-HOOK CONTRACTIONS.

Punish-ed-ment. Combine. Bank. Taken. At once
But once. Denominate-d. Religion. General-ly. Imagine-ary.
Generalize. Generalized. Continue-d. Continual-ly.
Continuous. Continuously. Connect-ed. Constitute-d.
Constitution. Constable. Begin, Organ. Begun, Again.
Began. Beginner. Organize. Organized. Organic.
Forgotten. Financial-ly. Divine-ity. Within. Reference.
Men. Man. Human. Opinion, Any one. No one.
None. Lengthen. Uniform-ity.

NOTE.—The N-Hook may be used before K, in many words, instead of the Ng-stem, as shown in the following illustrations:

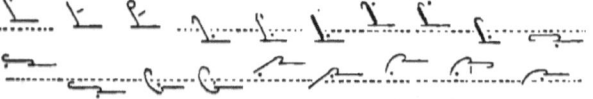

☞ *Write Exercise XIII. of the Speed-Book.*

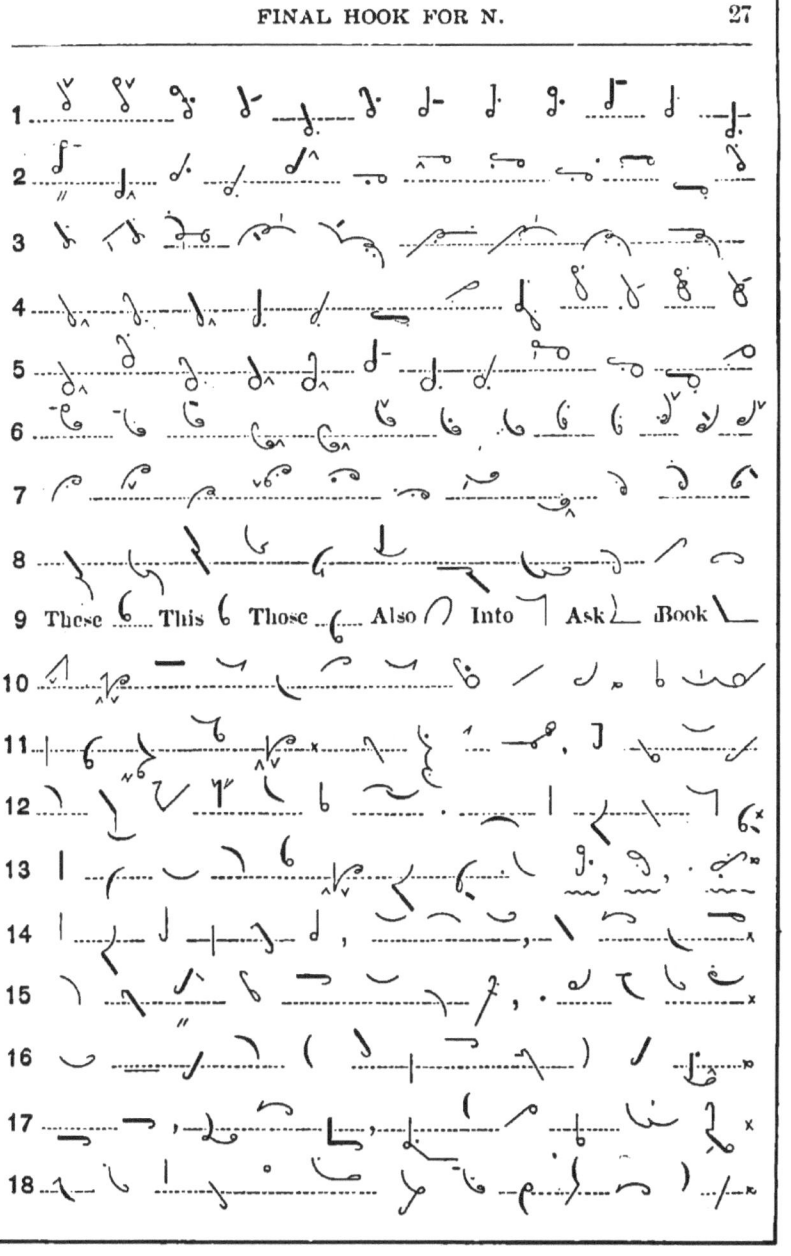

9 These ... This ... Those ... Also ... Into ... Ask ... Book

FINAL HOOK FOR F AND V.

Sec. 17. A small final hook, on the L-hook side of a straight stem, or a lengthened final hook on the inner side of a curved stem, indicates an added F or V. (*Lines 1-4.*)

a. S or Z is added to the F-hook by writing the circle within the hook. (*Line 5.*)

b. The F-hook is always read after the stem to which it is attached, and after any vowel or initial hook, but before a final circle. When F or V is the last consonant sound of a word, and is followed by a vowel, the stem must be used.

c. Phrasing.—The F-hook adds to a word-sign the word *Have, Of, Ever,* or *Live.* (*Line 6.*)

d. A small hook within the F-hook on curves, indicates N or Ng, and also adds the word *Been,* in phrasing. (*Line 6.*)

KEY TO LINE 6.—It-will-have-been. Ought-to-have-known. To-have-known. To-have-been. There-have. They-have. You-have. Part-of. Which-of-these. Forever. Have-ever. It-may-have-been. They-have-been.

F-HOOK CONTRACTIONS.

Poverty......Perform-ed, Hope to have\   Part of...\...,Performance\

Subjective-ly \ Whatever, Ought to have.l...Deform-ed-ity.l... Difficult-y l

Develope l   Advice, Advise-d...l.....Objective-ly....l......Suggestive-ly l

Govern-ed __ Government __ Refer / Thoughtful...l.....

☞ *Write Exercises XIV. and XV. of the Speed-Book.*

INITIAL HOOK FOR Y.

Sec. 18. A large initial hook, on the R-hook side of straight stems, or a long and narrow initial hook on the inner side of curves, adds the consonant sound of Y. This hook is used in phrasing only, and adds to a word-sign the word *You, Your, You are,* or *Year.* (*Line 11.*)

a. The Y-semi-circle may indicate the same words, where the hook-cannot be conveniently used. (*Line 11.*)

KEY TO LINE 11.—Do-you-not. Did-you-ever. Which-you-have. If-you-will. Have-you-seen. Should-you-say. May-you-not. For-your-own. What-year. What-were-you. Where-were-you. In-that-year.

☞ *Write Exercise XVI. of the Speed-Book.*

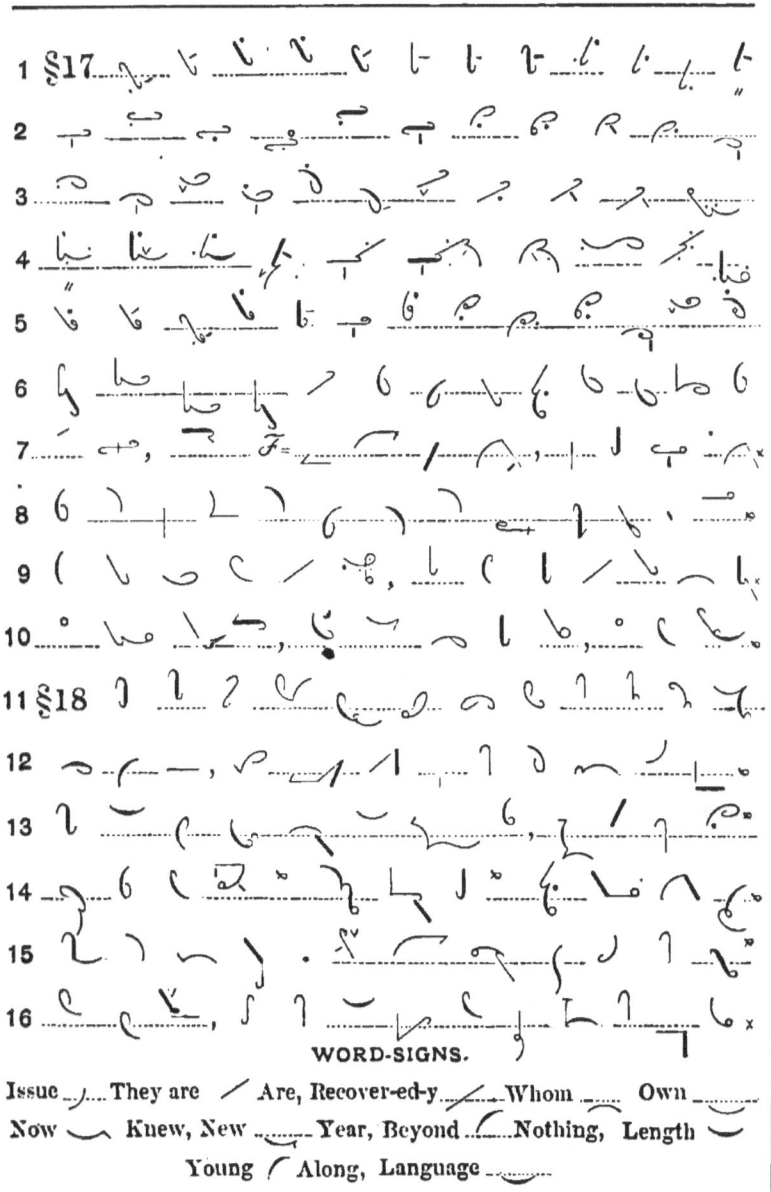

WORD-SIGNS.

Issue .... They are / Are, Recover-ed-y .... Whom ...... Own ....
Now ...... Knew, New .... Year, Beyond .... Nothing, Length ....
Young (Along, Language ....

INITIAL HOOK FOR W.

Sec. 19. A large initial hook, on the L-hook side of straight stems only, adds the sound of W, and is read after the stem but before any final hook, circle, or loop. (*Lines 1-3.*)

a. Phrasing.—The W-hook adds to a word-sign the word *We, Would, What, Whether, Way,* or *Away.* (*Line 4.*)

b. The W-semi-circle may indicate the same words, where the hook cannot be conveniently used. The semi-circle is also used for *Were.* (*Line 4.*)

KEY TO LINE 4.—Before-we-came. Did-we-not. Which-we-may-have. Can-we-not. Upon-what. By-what-means. About-what-time. But-whether-you-can. Part-way. Go-away. If-they-were. If-we-were.

☞ *Write Exercise XVII. of the Speed-Book.*

FINAL HOOK FOR TER, DER AND THER.

Sec. 20. A large final hook written in place of the N-hook, on any straight stem, adds to the stem the syllable Ter, Der, or Ther, to be read after the stem and after any vowel or initial hook, but before a final circle or N-Hook. (*Lines 5, 6.*)

a. A final Iss-circle, or a small hook for N, may be written within the Ter-hook. (*Line 6.*)

b. The final N-hook written within the Ter-hook, may be used for the affix -*ing.*

c. Phrasing.—The Ter-hook adds to any word-sign the word *Their, There* or *They are,* and occasionally the word *Other.* (*Line 7.*)

KEY TO LINE 7.—Upon-their. Put-their. By-their. Before-their. About-there. What-there-is. At-their. Did-their. Had-their. Which-their. Came-there. Can-there-be. Or-there. Each-other.

☞ *Write Exercise XVIII. of the Speed-Book.*

FINAL HOOK FOR M.

Sec. 21. A short, broad final hook, written in place of the F-hook on straight stems, and on the inner side of curves, adds the sound of M to the stem. This hook is read after the stem, and after any vowel or initial hook, but before a final circle or N-hook. (*Lines 8-16.*)

30

1 §19

2

3

4

W-HOOK CONTRACTIONS.

Bewilder-ed ⌇ Dwell-t-ing ʃ Quarter-ed ⌒ Question-ed ⌒

Acquiesce ⌒ Acquiesced ⌒ Railway ✓

5 §20

6

7

8 §21

9

10

11

12

13

14

15

16

a. A final Iss-circle, or a small hook for N, may be written within the M-hook. This N-hook may also be used for the
affix -*ing*. When M is the last consonant in a word, and is followed by a vowel, the stem is used. (*Line 1.*)

b. If two vowels occur between M and a preceding stem,
the M-stem is used, excepting such words as are illustrated in
line 2.

c. Phrasing.—The M-hook adds to a word-sign the word
May, Him, Time, Make or *My.* (*Line 3.*)

d. *Than, Been* or *Own*, is added by the small N-hook written within any final large or lengthened hook. (*Line 4.*)

KEY TO LINES 3 AND 4.—It-may-be. Which-may-be. Pay-him. By-
him. About-him. For-him. With-him. Saw-him. Show-him. At-that-
time. A-different-time. Did-you-make-known. In-my-room.

Better-than. Rather-than. Ever-have-been. Have-ever-been. Shall-
have-been. Upon-their-own. Upon-my-own. At-their-own. At-my-own.
Had-their-own. Had-my-own.

☞ *Write Exercise XIX. of the Speed-Book.*

FINAL HOOK FOR TION.

Sec. 22. The syllables Tion, Sion, etc., are expressed by a
small circle and back-hook similar to the expedient for Sn.
(*See Sec. 8, g, h*). A small circle may be written within the back-
hook to add S. The syllable Tion may be added to an N-hook,
on a straight stem, by changing that hook to a circle and con-
tinuing the stroke to form a back-hook ; and another circle for
S may be written within the back-hook. (*Lines 6-12.*)

a. Tion may be indicated after the D-stem and an F-hook,
by a small hook outside of .the F-hook ; but when two vowels
immediately precede this syllable, in such cases, Ish with the
N-hook is used for Tion. (*Line 12.*)

b. In such words as *dictionary, stationer, national*, the back-
hook is omitted. (*Lines 13, 14.*)

c. The past tense of verbs ending with Tion, is indicated
by halving the stem immediately preceding that syllable. In
words ending with -*ate* following Tion, a half-length N is used
after the circle, instead of the back-hook. (*See Section 23.*)
(*Line 15.*)

1 ...

2 ...

3 ...

4 ...

M-HOOK CONTRACTIONS.

Discriminate-d ⌡⌐ Commission-ed ⌐ Commissioner ⌐ Criminate-d ⌐

Familiar-ly ⌐ Familiarize-d ⌐ Family ⌐ Themselves ⌐ Minimum ⌐

Memorandum ⌐ Memoranda ⌐ Sometime ⌐ Nominate-d ⌐

5 ...

6 §22 ...

7 ...

8 ...

9 ...

10 ...

11 ...

12 ...

13 ...

14 ...

15 ...

d. The termination S-tion, in such words as *position*, *physician*, is indicated by a large circle and baçk-hook ; and a final circle may be written within the back-hook. (*Line 1.*)

e. S-tion is added to an N-hook, by changing the hook to a large circle and adding a back-hook ; and a final circle may be written within the back-hook. (*Line 2.*)

f. In words ending with *-est* or *-ist*, following Tion, the syllable may be indicated by a small loop added after the circle, or by using a half-length S. (*Line 2.*)

☞ *Write Exercise XX. of the Speed-Book.*

HALVING TO ADD T OR D.

Sec. 23. Making any stem half-length, except as stated in this section, adds to it the sound of T or D. The added sound is read after the stem, and after all vowels and hooks, but before a final circle or loop. (*Lines 3-9.*)

a. Words containing a second-place vowel, with no other stem than L, R, M or N, when halved to add the sound of D, are written *through* the line, to distinguish them from similar words ending with the sound of T ; but when such words end with a hook, the sound of D may be indicated by shading the hook.

b. Half-length stems are written below the line, for the third position.

c. A half-length stem must not be joined to another stem, except where its length can be readily distinguished.

d. Ray is seldom halved to add D, except when hooked, or when preceded by F, V, M or L. (*Line 10.*)

e. The syllable *-tive* is usually indicated by a V-stem following a half-length. (*Line 11.*)

f. Phrasing.—Halving any word-sign, or the last stem of an outline, adds the word *It* or *The*, and occasionally the word *To*. (*Lines 12, 13.*)

KEY TO LINES 12, 13.—Take-it-away. Did-it-mean. If-it-had-not-been. For-which-it-was. Can-it-be. If-it-were. Is-it-not. After-it-was. Shall-it-be-said. Where-it-was. May-it-not-be. Whether-it-is-or-not.
Upon-the-occasion. About-the-same. At-the-time. Charge-the-amount. For-the-sum. Of-the. With-the-details. From-the-time. What-were-the-means. Go-to-him.

NOTE.—A dot at the beginning of a stem indicates the prefix Com or or Con. See (*) on page 35. A dot at the *end* of a stem, indicates Ing.

1

2

TION-HOOK CONTRACTIONS.

Occupation ...... Compassion ...... Passion...... Opposition ...... Position

Possession...... Contention ...... Attention Tension Decision ......

Denomination ...... Condensation Conditional-ly ...... Additional-ly ......

Continuation ...... Connection ...... Actionable-y ...... Organization ......

Formation ...... Conviction ...... Recollection Resolution ......

Nomination ...... Information ...... Incision ...... Institution ......

3 §23

4

5

6

7

8

9

10

11

12

13

g. Halving a pronoun or adverb, adds the word *Did.* Halving any preposition which is written with a curved stem, adds the word *What.* (*Line 1.*)

KEY TO LINE 1.—What-did-you-mean.   Which-did-you-get.   When-did-you-go. We-did. You-did. If-they-did. He-did-not. She-did-not-say-that. Whether-he-did-or-not. Where-did-you-see-him. From-what-time.

☞ *Write Exercises XXI. and XXII. of the Speed-Book.*

LENGTHENING FOR TER, DER, AND THER.

Sec. 24. Lengthening a curved stem, or a straight stem which ends with a hook, adds the syllable Ter, Der, or Ther. The added syllable is read after all vowels and hooks, but before a final circle. (*Lines 2-9.*)

a. The first half of a lengthened stem is placed in the position indicated by the leading vowel of the word, in accordance with the rule at section 4, *b*, in the same manner as if it were a single stem.

b. Phrasing.—Lengthening a stem, adds to it the word *Their, There* or *They are,* and sometimes the word *Other.* (*Line 10.*)

KEY TO LINE 10.—If-there-has-been. For-there-is-not. Have-there-been. Thought-there-might-be. Of-their. So-there-was. May-there. In-there. I-think-there-is. Whether-there-is-or-not. When-they-are.

☞ *Write Exercise XXIII. of the Speed-Book.*

SPECIAL RULES AND SUGGESTIONS.

Sec. 25.—a. When a regular verb in the present tense ends with a half length stem, the syllable -*ed* may be added for the past tense by an inclined final tick struck at a distinct angle with the half-length or with its final hook. A tick may also be used after a loop for the same purpose. (*Lines 11-13.*)

b. Words of the same part of speech and containing the same consonants, must be distinguished by vocalization, or by difference of position or outline. When two such words belong in the same position, the most frequently occurring one should have the preference; but where there is little or no difference in that respect, preference should be given to one containing a diphthong, or an accented long vowel. (*See p. 64.*)

1.

HALF-LENGTH CONTRACTIONS.

Particular. Opportunity, Pretty Except Accept Expand

Expend-iture Decreed, According to Built-d-ing Able to

Toward Gentlemen Gentleman Quite Could Good

Guilty Neglect Negligent Somewhat Mental-ly

Not, Need Under, Hundred Nature, Hand Individual-ly

Nevertheless Notwithstanding Understood Understand

Anybody Nobody Neighborhood Immediate -ly

2 §24

3

4

5

6

7

8

9

10

11 §25

12

13

c. Words having peculiar outlines, and most words containing more than two upright or inclined stems, may be written on the line. (*Line 1.*)

d. No hook, circle, or loop, can be used at the end of a word, when the sound indicated by it is immediately preceded and followed by vowels.

e. As far as possible, derivatives should be written with outlines similar to those of their primitives, and usually in the same position.

f. The sound of Sh is sometimes indicated by the circle or loop, as in *accomplish, negotiate.* (*Line 2.*)

g. When T or D is followed by the consonant sound of Y, both sounds may be expressed by Chay or Jay. (*Line 2.*)

h. In words ending with K-tion following T or D, K may generally be omitted. K may also be omitted in many words in which K-tion follows other consonants ; and other letters are omitted in some cases, as indicated in lines 3 to 5.

i. Foreign sounds are indicated by striking a light waved line through stems most nearly representing them. (*Line 6.*)

j. The termination -*ure* may be indicated by the stem Y ; also, by the Ter-hook, by Chay or Jay with the R-hook, by the Str-loop, or by lengthening a curved stem. (*Line 7.*)

k. The semi-circles for the coalescents W and Y may be written by the side of a stem, in the position of a vowel, thus indicating both the consonant and the vowel which follows it. In such cases the W-semi-circle opens to the right to indicate a dot vowel, and to the left to indicate a dash vowel ; and the Y-semi-circle opens upward for a dot vowel, and downward for a dash vowel. The semi-circles may be shaded for long vowels, and made light for short vowels, if desired. (*Line 8.*)

l. The back-hook after a circle may often be used to indicate the affix -*ing*, but care should be taken that the resulting outline be not of such form as to be mistaken for a different word. In words containing more than one stem, the N-hook may also be used for the same purpose, the same precaution being taken. (*Line 9.*)

☞ *Write Exercise XXIV. of the Speed-Book.*

1

2

3

4

5

6 (*Ger.*) Einig .... Ich ⊢ (*Fr.*) In ⤳ .en .... bon

7

COALESCENTS.

WĒĒ | WĀ | WAH | WAW | WŌ | WŌŌ |
YĒĒ | YĀ | YAH | YAW | YŌ | YŌŌ |

8

9

10

11

HALF-LENGTH CONTRACTIONS.

Quantity .... Acquaint-ance ⊂, Contract .... Trade ꓶ Attract ....

Direct, Day or two ꓶ Effect ⤳ Affect, Fact .... Frequent-ly ....

Convict .... Authority .... With regard to .... Without regard to ....

Import-ant .... Imports-ance .... Independent ⤳ Intelligent ....

Subjected ꓻ Consequent-ly .... Examined .... Mentioned ⤳

Remarked .... Measured ꓶ In regard to .... Water .... As regards ....

Year or two .... Yet ꓷ Behind .... Movement ....

m. Phrasing.—It was stated in section 23, *f*, that the word *To* is sometimes added to a word by halving. *To* is generally indicated, however, by writing the preceding and following words near each other, rather than by halving; but where *To* is followed by a word which may be added to it by a hook, circle, loop, or other expedient, in accordance with the phrasing rules heretofore given, the better practice is to write the word-sign for *To*, with the subsequent word so added. (*Lines 14–18, page 47.*)

☞ *Write Exercise XXV. of the Speed-Book.*

PREFIXES AND AFFIXES.

Sec. 26. One of the most important methods of abbreviation in Phonetic Shorthand, is that of using certain signs for frequently occurring prefixes and affixes, rules for which are given in this section. Illustrations of the use of these rules will be found on page 43.

Prefixes.—1. The prefix *Accom* is indicated by the stem K, joined to the remainder of the word. (*Line 1.*)

· 2. *Com, Con,* or *Cog,* is generally indicated by a dot at the beginning of the first stem of an outline. In some words, however, it is better to use K with the N-hook for *Con.* (*Line 2.*)

3. In the middle of a word, *Com, Con,* or *Cog,* is indicated by disconnecting the outline at the point where the syllable occurs. (*Line 3.*)

4. *Contra, Counter,* by an inclined tick written in place of the Con-dot; by a half-length K with the N-hook, followed by Ar or Ray as is most convenient; or, in a few instances, by T with the R-hook, preceded by the Con-dot. (*Line 4.*)

5. *For, Fore,* by F, joined to the remainder of the word. (*Line 5.*)

6. *In, Un,* by the N-stem; or, when followed by Iss, by an initial back-hook, if the N-stem will not readily join. (*Line 6.*)

7. *Inter, Intro, Enter,* by a half-length N, either joined or disjoined. If disjoined, it should be written to the succeeding stem in the position of the first vowel of the prefix. (*Line 7.*)

8. *Magna, Magni*, by a disjoined M, written over or near the remainder of the word. *Magnify*, and its derivatives are written MG. (*Line 8.*)

9. *Rel*, by the stem Ray with the L-hook. (*Line 9.*)

10. *Self*, by the syllable written in full, where convenient. In other cases, by the Iss-circle, as shown in line 10.

11. *There* should always be written with the stem Ray, but in such words as *thereupon, therefore, thereafter*, the inclination of the Ray should be so changed as to bring the remainder of the word in its proper position. (*Line 11.*)

Affixes.—12. *Ble, Bly*, are indicated by B and the L-hook; or where the hook cannot be used conveniently, by B alone. (*Line 12.*)

13. *Bleness*, by B with the L-hook and final Iss, disjoined and written through the line. (*Line 13.*)

14. *Ed*, by halving the last stem of an outline ; by a half-length T or D, joined or disjoined, after a full-length stem : or by an inclined tick after a loop or a half-length stem, as provided in section 25, *a*. (*Line 14.*)

15. *Ential, Entially*, by Sh following the N-hook. *Essential* and *essentially* are written SN. (*Line 15.*)

16. *Ever*, by the F-hook ; *Soever*, by the circle and V-stem. (*Line 16.*)

17. *For, Fore, Form*, by F joined to the preceding portion of the word. (*Line 17.*)

18. *Ful, Fully*, by the F-hook, except when the affix follows a circle or hook, in which case it is indicated by the stem F. (*Line 18.*)

19. *Fullness*, by F followed by Iss, written through the line near the preceding portion of the word. (*Line 19.*)

20. *Ing* is better indicated by the Ing-stem, in many cases. After the Tr- or M-hook, or after the F-hook on a curved stem, it is indicated by a small hook within the larger one. In other cases, it is indicated by a dot at the end of the .

last stem of an outline. In such words as *exceedingly*, the Ing-dot is placed at the end of the last stem preceding L. See, also, section 10, *b*, and section 25, *l*. (*Line 20.*)

21. A perpendicular or horizontal tick, in place of the Ing-dot, indicates the syllable Ing followed by *a*, *an* or *and*. An inclined tick, in the same position, indicates *ing* followed by *the*. (*Line 21.*)

22. When a word ends with *ing*, it is often convenient to indicate the affix by beginning the next word near the Ing-dot place, or by striking the first stem of the succeeding word through the last stem of the word to which the affix belongs. (*Line 22.*)

23. *Ings* may be written with Ing and the small circle, or by making a circle in place of the Ing-dot. (*Line 23.*) _

24. *L-ty* or *R-ty*, in such words as *formality*, *popularity*, may be expressed by detaching the preceding stem. In some cases, these terminations may be indicated by halving Lay or Ray, or by halving a stem bearing the L- or R-hook. *Bility*, as well as *Ble* and *Bly*, is expressed after a circle by the stem B. (*Line 24.*)

25. *Lessness*, by Lay and the Iss-circle, disjoined. (*Line 25.*)

26. *Mental*, *Mentality*, by a half-length M with the N-hook. (*Line 26.*)

27. *Ology*, *Ological*, by J, either joined or disjoined. (*Line 27.*)

28. *Ography*, *Ographer*, by G. with or without the R-hook. (*Line 28.*)

29. *Self*, *Selves*, by the syllable written out, except in a few cases where it is more convenient to indicate the affix by a small circle. (*Line 29.*)

30. *Ship*, by Sh, either joined or disjoined. (*Line 30.*)

31. *Ly*, by El, or by Lay joined or disjoined. (*Line 31*)

☞ *Write Exercise XXVI. of the Speed-Book.*

NOTE.—When an outline is disconnected, the different parts must be written very near each other.

1		Accomplish / Accomplishment / Accommodation
2		Combination / Conscience / Contour
3		Unconditional-ly / Incumbent / Recognition
4		Contravene / Counterplea / Contradiction
5		Forenoon / Formidable-y / Forbid
6		Inspiration / Insolvent / Unconsidered
7		Introduce / Introversion / Entertain
8		Magnanimous / Magnesia / Magna Charta
9		Relation / Realization / Reliable
10		Self-esteem / Selfish / Self-defense
11		Thereupon / Therefor-e / Thereafter
12		Notable-y / Feasible-y / Profitable-y
13		Changeableness / Tractableness / Curableness
14		Located / Imitated / Invited
15		Credential / Deferential / Inferential
16		Whatever / Wherever / Whenever
		Whosoever / Howsoever / Whatsoever
17		Therefor-e / Inform / Platform
18		Careful-ly / Cheerful-ly / Thoughtful-ly
		Successful-ly / Harmful / Painful
19		Cheerfulness / Hopefulness / Wilfulness
20		Being / Tottering / Teaming
		Moving / Going / Accordingly
21		Taking a / Forming a / Giving a
		Taking the / Seeing the / Giving the
22		Storing goods / Receiving them / Having done
23		Complainings / Pleadings / Proceedings
24		Formality / Popularity / Feasibility
		Liability / Majority / Vitality
25		Thoughtlessness / Carelessness / Fearlessness
26		Rudimental / Fundamental / Instrumental
27		Theology / Physiology / Geology
28		Geography-er / Biography-er / Stenography-er
29		Myself / Of itself / Themselves
30		Friendship / Hardship / Ownership
31		Kindly / Suddenly / Early

PHRASING.

Sec. 27. The student will have noticed that there are two kinds of phrase-writing taught in the rules heretofore given—Simple Phrasing, which is the joining of two or more outlines; and Group Phrasing, which is the representation of phrases by the use of hooks, circles, or loops, attached to a word-sign, or by the halving or lengthening principles. As to either method, the following directions should be carefully observed :

a. Such words only should be joined as have a close grammatical relation to each other.

b. If the elements of a phrase cannot be easily and readily joined, or if for any reason they would not be distinct when joined, the combination should not be made.

c. Two distinct phrases should not be joined together.

d. Two large hooks should not be written on the same side of a straight stem, in phrasing, as they would have a tendency to curve the stem ; and no hook can be used to add a word to a stem which is halved or lengthened for a preceding word. .

e. Unusual phrases, as *come what will*, should not be joined.

f. When a phrase begins with the tick word-sign for *A, An, And, I, He,* or *The,* the second word of the phrase should be written in position, and not the tick.

g. When a phrase begins with the tick for *Awe, All, Already,* or *On,* or with the circle for *Is* or *His,* or with a first-position horizontal or half-length word-form, such tick, circle, horizontal or half-length may be slightly raised or lowered when joined to another word which begins above the line of writing.

h. In all other cases, the first word of a phrase should be written in the position it would occupy if standing alone.

i. A word or letter may be omitted from a phrase-sign, or changed in form, if the context will clearly and certainly suggest it. (*Lines 1, 2, page 47.*)

NOTE.—In a very few instances, it may be found that a word-sign cannot be distinguished readily if written out of its natural position in a phrase-sign. No general rule can be given to govern such cases, but the student must learn, by practice in reading, to avoid such combinations.

j. Special phrasing contractions may be made, where difficult or lengthy combinations of words occur frequently in a report. (*Line 3.*)

k. Simple Phrasing.—The simplest phrase-sign is made by joining two or more words without change of form. (*Line 4.*)

l. Words forming part of a complete phrase may be joined, and the remainder written separately, if necessary on account of especial difficulty of junction. (*Line 5.*)

m. Group Phrasing.—*Having* may be added by the F-Hook and the Ing-dot, but in most cases it is sufficiently indicated by the hook alone. (*Line 6.*)

n. After a final circle or hook, or after a half-length curve, *Their* or *There* is added by a heavy tick. (*Line 6.*)

☞ *Write Exercise XXVII. of the Speed-Book.*

o. *Than, Been, Own,* or *One,* is indicated by a back-hook, after a circle or loop. (*Line 7.*)

p. *It* may be indicated by a final tick, struck at an acute angle with any final hook or half-length stem. (*Line 7.*)

q. If for any reason *Him* cannot be conveniently indicated by the M-hook, it should be written with Hay, though it may be represented by a P-tick after a final hook. (*Line 8.*)

r. *Himself* may often be indicated by the M-hook and final circle. *Myself* must never be written with the M-hook. (*Line 8.*)

☞ *Write Exercise XVIII. of the Speed-Book.*

s. *One* may be added by the N-hook to either of the following words : *At, But, Each, Which, Some, Any, No, Long, Every, Either, Other, Only.* (*Line 9.*)

t. When an outline ends with Iss, enlarging the circle adds to it the word *Is, His, As,* or *Has.* (*Line 10.*)

u. *In* or *In the* is prefixed by an initial back-hook to a word or phrase beginning with Iss, if the N-stem cannot be used as conveniently. (*Line 10.*)

v. *Should* may be indicated by the Ray-tick, if that can be more easily joined than Sh. When preceded by *I, He* or *You,* or when used initially, the tick must rest upon the line. (*Line 11.*)

w. Very careful writers may use the small hooks and circles on the tick word-signs. (*Line 12.*)

x. *Of* and *Of the* are generally omitted between two nouns which are joined in a phrase-sign. (*Line 13.*)

y. *Or* is implied between two sets of figures, when the second set is written above the line. *And* or *To* is implied when the second set is written below the line. (*Line 13.*)

☞ *Write Exercise XXIX. of the Speed-Book.*

KEY TO PHRASES ON PAGE 47.—1. Most-likely. Ought-to-have-been. Ought-not-to-have-been. It-seems-to-be. Refresh-your-recollection. Yes-or-no. Five-or-six. Great-deal. Couldn't-tell. In-order-to-have. 2. Night-time. The-other. I-am-not-sure. It-must-have-been. Did-you-have-any-conversation. Bear-in-mind. In-earnest. In-reply-to-your-letter. Do-you-not-remember. Once-or-twice. Eternal-life.
3. New-York-Central-Railroad. German-Insurance-Company. Mutual-Life-Insurance-Company. Where-do-you-reside. Where-do-you-live. How-long-have-you-lived. In-Rochester. Entitled-to-recover. Guilt-or-innocence. What-is-your-business.
4. It-was. It-has-been. It-may-be. Upon-that-subject. Do-so. Shall-be. Hand-in-hand. Will-be-certain. It-has-not-been. Is-not-inclined. That-which may-be.
5. It-must-not-be supposed. If-that could-be. There may-not-be. If-they should-come. Which-has-been chosen. May-require adjustment.
6. After-having. For-having. In-having. With-having. Upon-having. About-having. Gives-their. Puts-their. Knows-there. Been-there. Gone-there. Done-their. Affect-their. Note-their.
7. Less-than. That-there-has-been. For-it-has-been. By-his-own. Find-it. Around-it. Maintained-it. Renewed-it. They-did-it. Why-did-it.
8. Bid-him. Taught-him. Affect-him. Lend-him. Mind-him. Around-him. Offend-him. Attend-him. Dun-him. By-himself. For-himself. With-himself.
9. At-one. But-one. Each-one. Which-one. Some-one. Any-one. No-one. Long-one. Every-one. Either-one. Other-one. Only-one.
10. What-is-his-name. It-is-as-much. Enlarges-his. Where-is-his. He-tells-us. In-the-same. In-the-spring. In-the-street. In-the-same-place. In-the-supreme-court. In-the-same-room.
11. It-should-be. It-should-not-have-been. Which-should-have. We-should-not. I-should-not-be. He-should-not-know. Should-not-suppose. Should-have-said. You-should-have-seen. You-should-not-be. You-should-not-have-been.
12. All-were. All-will. All-of. All-have-been. All-is-done. All-has-been. Who-will. Who-were. Who-have. I-have-been. He-is. He-has. Is-he. Has-he. On-his-own.
13. What-time-of-day. What-time-of-night. Piece-of-land. Acts-of-congress. Bill-of-sale.—Bills-of-sale. 25-or-26. 25-or-30. Between-7-and-10. From 5-to-6-hundred-dollars.
14. Charley is-to-be-sent-to-New-York tomorrow-to-meet-his-mother, and-he will go with-her on-Saturday to-your-brother's house.
15. After-having-been advised as-to-his condition, they-decided not-to-remove him at-present, and-he-remains in-the-same-room where-you saw-him today.
16. Our general-agent expects-to-be at-your-place next-week, and-will call upon-you and explain the-matter fully.
17, 18. Complete lists of-the word-signs and-contractions of-the system are given in-the-pages which follow this-exercise. The student is-advised-to-examine these lists with care, and-to-write out and-commit-to-memory those which he-has-not already learned.

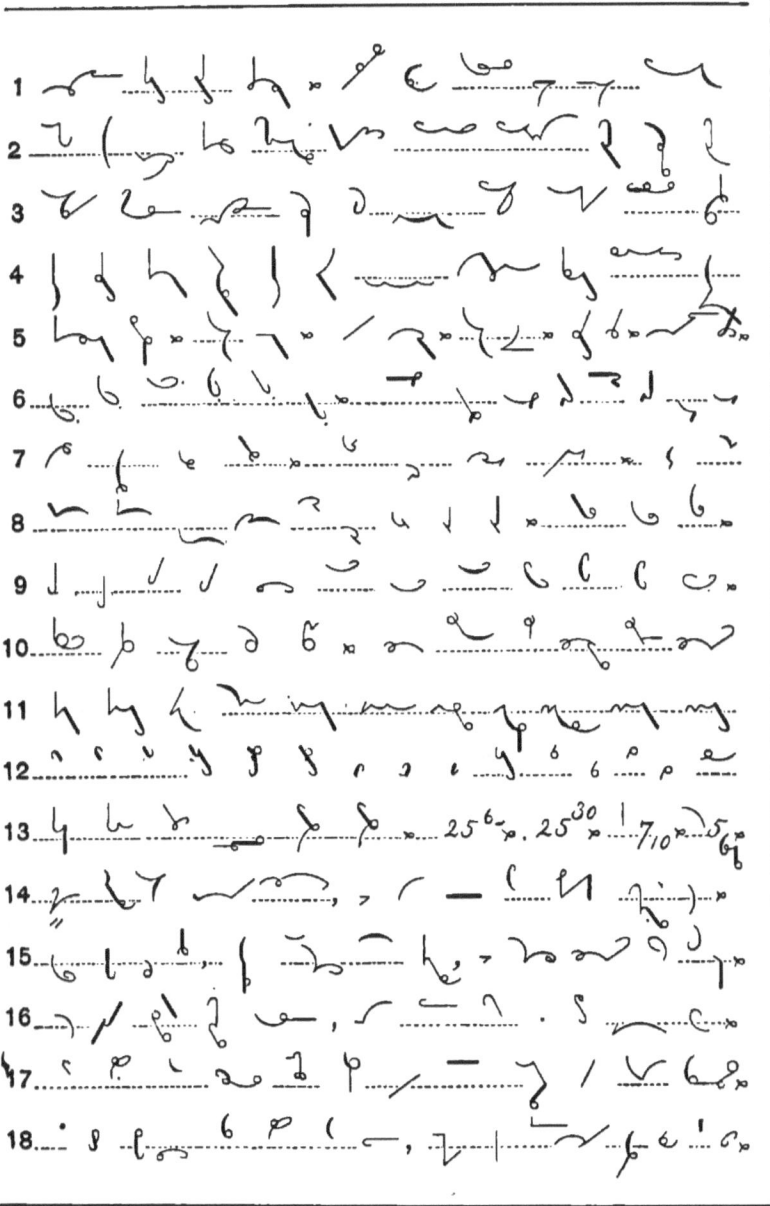

WORD-SIGNS.

The ticks for TO, HOW, and SHOULD, and the circles for AS and HAS, are used in phrasing only. The word-signs for ON, SHOULD, and HOW, are written upward.

....The	....All	....Awe, Already	....He	....Is, His
. A	/ Who	ı Oh, Owe	....On	o As , Has
...Ah	\ Two, Too	....I, High	/ Should	....Is there
. An, And	\ To	ᴄ First	...How	....H-as there

	Upon, Property, Occupy		Ease, Easy
	Up, Hope, Pay		Was, Owes
	Put, Part, Party, Happy		Has, As, Whose
	Be, By, Buy		She, Wish
	Before		Shall, Show
	About		Should, Issue
	What, Ought, Talk, Between		
	At, Take, It		Usual, Usually
	Out, To, But, Took [Dollar		
	Did, Differ-ed-ent-ence,		While, Ill, Lie
	Do, Defendant, Day		Will, Well, Low
	Had, Add		Allow, Whole,
	Watch, Each		From, Here, Hear
	Which, Change		Where, Were, Her
	Charge, Much		Our, Hour
	Object-ed, Adjoin-ed		Or [Recollect
	Agent, Age		There, Their, They are,
	Judge, Large, Advantage		Recover, Recovery, Are
	[Week		Me, My, Time
	Common, Commit-ted-tee,		May
	Company, Come, Came		Am, Whom
	Can, Accompany-ied, [County		In, Any
	Give, Given		No, Know
	Go, Gave, Against,		Knew, Own
	Ago, Together		Not, Need
	If, Wife, Form		Under, Hundred
	For, Forget, Forgot		Nature, Hand
	After, Half		Year, Beyond
	Of, Live		Yes, Young
	Ever, Heavy		You, Your, You are
	Have, Above		We, Why, Without,
	Thought		Whether, Way [Wheel
	Worth, Oath, Month		Would, Away
	Thank, Youth		Him
	With, Thy		When
	They, Though, Worthy		How
	That, Thou		Think, Long, Thing
	See, Saw		Nothing, Among, Length
	So, Say, Us		Language, Along
	House, Sue		

48

CONTRACTIONS AND WORD-FORMS.

SIMPLE CONTRACTIONS.

Public-ly-ish-ed
Publication
Peculiar-ly-ity

Perpendicular-ly
Pecuniary
Operation

Portion [ison
Apportion, Compar-
Became, Become

By virtue of
Bond and mortgage
Better

Better than
At any rate
Technical-ly-ity

At last
Dignify-ied-ty
Democrat-ic-cy

Domestic
Downward
Doctrine-al

Determine
Determined
Determination

Danger
Dangerous
Declare

Declaration
Demonstrate
Demonstration

Chattel mortgage
Changeable-y
Chargeable-y

January
Agency
Advantageous

Capable-y-ity
Acknowledge
Acknowledged

Acknowledgement
Commonly
Common law

Commercial-ly
Catholic
Roman Catholic

October
Quite
Could

Altogether
Good deal
Good while

Few
February
Former

Formerly
Forgiven
Affidavit

Effect
Affect, Fact
Convict

Verse, Various
Versed
Version, Variation

Especial-ly
Essential-ly
Assume

Assumption
Assignment
Establish-ed

Establishment
Eastern, Astronomy
East and West

Easterly
Eastward
Legislate-d-or-ure

Legislation
Represent-ed
Representative

Representation
Original-ly-ate-d
Regular-ly

Republic-ish-ed
Republican
Regeneration

Require
Required
Architect-ure-al

Argue-ment
Reform-ed
Reformation

Retrospect
Wherefore
Heretofore

Arrangement [rive
Revolve-d-er, Ar-
Reverend, Revenue

Revolution
Reorganize
Import-ant

Importance
Impart
Imperfect

Improvement
Mechanic-al
Mutual-ly

Maturity
From time to time
Manufacture-d

Manufactory
Manufacturer
Immediate-ly

Movement
Material-ly
Any other

No other
New
Now

Any way
Anything
Envelope

Anybody
Nobody
Neighborhood

Inquire-y
Inquired
In accordance with

Engage-d
Negotiated
Inform-ed

Information
Involve-d
November, Never

Anniversary
Involution [tial-ly
Influential-ly, Ini-

Nevertheless
Independent-ly
Intelligence

Intelligent
Notify
Until

Entire
Natural-ly
Undertake

Undertaken
Undertook
Individual-ly

INITIAL CIRCLES.

Is, His
As, Has
Is his, His is

As has, As is
And so forth
Speak, Speech

Spoke, Special-ly
Expect-ed
Spoken

Exception
Expectation
Expense-ive-ly

Expanse-ive-ly
Expand
Subject, Subpoena

Subjective-ly
Subjection
Subjected

Satisfy-ied
Satisfies
Satisfaction

Satisfactory
Satisfactorily
Circumstantial-ly,
[Extension

Circumstance, Ex-
Setoff [tensive-ly
Set forth

Consist
System
Considerate

Situate-d
Situation
Suggest-ed-ion

Suggestive-ly
Consequence
Consequential-ly

Consequent-ly [ied
Signature, Signify-
Significant-ly

Significance
Signification
Sufficient

Sufficiency
Several
Southeast

Southeastern
Southern
Certainly

Certify
Certification
Circumference

Somebody
Sometime
Some of the time

Somewhat
Cemetery
Similar-ity

Similarly
Some one, Summon
Examine

Examined
Examination
Southwesterly

Southwestern
Single-ular-ly-ity
Singly

FINAL CIRCLES AND LOOPS.

Possible-y-ity
Positive-ly
Up stairs

Possess
Business
Observe-d

Observance
Observation [gages
Bonds and mort-

Bondsman
Advertise
Advertised

Advertisement
Advertiser
Testament

Testify
Testified
Testimony

December
Destruction
Discharge-d

Disadvantage
Administer
Administrate

Administrative
Administration
Administrator

Administratrix
Discover-ed-y
Discontinue-d

Disconnect-ed
Disorganize
Disorganized

Disorganization
Discriminate-d
Discrimination

Dissimilar-ity
Conditional-ly
Additional-ly

Disclaim-ed
Disqualify
Disqualification

Down stairs
Religious
Because

Actionable-y
Expend-iture
Exchange-d

Counsel-cil
Custom
Customer-ary

Accustom
Organism
Executor-y

Executrix
Extraordinary-ily
Efficient

Efficiency   [geon
Physician and Sur-
Thousand-th

These
This
Those

Reason
Almost
Most of the time

Mistake
Mistaken
Mistook

Misgovern-ed
Mr.
Mrs.

Misses
Messenger
Mention

Mentioned
Influence
Influenced

Influences
Next, Commenced
Inconsiderate

Insignificant
Inasmuch
Institute

Institution
Inconsistent
Instead

Next day
Next week
Next time

Next month
Next year
Indispensible-y

Interest
Interested
Anticipate

Anticipation
Understood
Understand

Notwithstanding
Intersection
Western

Westerly
Once more
Once or twice

R-HOOK.

Appear, Proper
Upper, Purpose
Practice

Practiced
Practical-ly
Practicable-y

Perhaps, Propose
Probable-y-ity
Profit

Particular, Pride
Opportunity, Pretty
Proud

Project-ed
Projection
Privilege

Person
Personal-ly [fessor
Perfect-ed-ly, Pro-

Proof, Prove
Approve-al
Perfection

Proficient-cy
Comprehend-ed
Preponderate-d,
[Principal-ly

Apprehend-ed.
Comprehension
Comprehensive-ly,
[Appearance

Apprehensive-ly
Preponderance
Properly

Preserve-d
Preservation
Preservative

Liberty
Member, Remember,
Brother, Number

Brother in law
Remembrance
Brethren

Transient
Internal-ly
Truth

True
Eternal-ly-ity
Controversy

Trustworthy
Transform-ed
Transfer-red

Treasure-r
Treasury
Contract, Tried

Trade, Tract, To-
Attract   [ward
Attraction

Dear
Doctor
During, Dark

Drink
Drunk
Drank, Darken

Direction
Duration
Direct, Day or two

Darkens, Darkness
Derive
Derivative

Charity
Adjourn-ed
Adjournment

Jury, Larger, Junior
Juryman
Jurisprudence

Jurisdiction
Decree
Care, Occur

Accrue, Car, Cure
Correct
Corrective

Correction
Corrector
Christian-ity

Character
Characterize
Characterized

Characteristic
Occurrence   [to
Decreed, According

Occurred   [Cured
Accrued, Cared,
Degree, Agree

Agriculture-al
Great deal
Great while

Grand jury
Greater
Greater than

Frequency
Furnish-ed
Frequent-ly

Furniture
Over
Every, Very

Verdict
Converse
Conversed

Conversation
Avert
Averse

Everybody
Everything
Everywhere

Authorize
Authorized
Authorization

Authority
Authoritative
Either

Other
Otherwise
Either one

Other one
Either way
Other way

On either hand
On the other hand
With regard to

With relation to
With reference to
With respect to

As regards
Measure
Measured

Lawyer
Learned
Learnéd

Lord
Railroad
Error

Remark, Mere
Remarked
Merchant

Merchandise
Mercantile
Mortgage-d

Near, Nor
Manner
In relation to

In order to
In regard to
In reference to

In respect to
In respect of
In reply

In writing
Handwriting
North and South

Northern
Northeast
Northeastern

Northwesterly
Northwestern
Longer

Without regard to
Without relation to
One or two

Work
Workman
Workmanship

Workmanlike
Younger
Year or two

L-HOOK.

Comply
Compel, People
Apply

Completion
Complication
Application

Applicable-y-ity
Compliance
Appliance

Plaintiff   [Plenty
Complaint-ed,
Applicant

Belong-ed
Believe-d
Build-ing, Built

Able to
Obligation
Blank

Balance
Balanced
At length

At all, It will
At all events
At least

ſ	ʃ	ʃ	Deliver-ed-y Deliverance Delinquent-cy
ʃ	⁄	⁄	Diligent Children Child
⁄	ſ	⌐	Challenge-d Angel Angelic
	⌐		Largely Equal, Call, Kill Claim-ed, Coal
	⌐₀	⌐₀	Clerk, Cool Equalize Equalized
⌐℮	⌐	⌐⊃	Equalization Collect Collective
⌐℮	⌐⊃	⌐ₒ	Collection Collector Qualification
⌐	⌐	⌐ₒ	Guilt-y, Gild Neglect, Gold Negligence
⌐	⌐	C	Negligent Afflict Affliction
C	C	⁄	Philanthropy-ic Voluntary Rely, Real-ly
⁄	⁄	⁄	Rail, Roll Rule Real estate

CIRCLE AND HOOK COMBINATIONS.

⁊	⁊	⁊	Superficial-ly Experiment-ed-al Surprise
⁊	⁊	⁊	Express Suppress Superintend-ent
⁊	⁊	⁊	Expression Suppression Experience
⁊	⁊	⁊	Experienced Inexperience Inexperienced
ſ	ſ	ſ	Explain Explained Explanation
⁊	⁊	⁊	External-ly, Strength Extra Stranger

⁊	⁊	ℓ	Extravagant-ce-ly Instruct-ed Instructive
ℒ	ℒ	⁊	Instruction Instrument-al-ly Consider-able-y
ℒ	⁊	ℒ	Consideration Inconsiderable-y Inconsideration
⁊	σ	σ⁓	Unconsidered Describe-d Descriptive
σℯ	σ	σ⁓	Description Prescribe-d Prescriptive
σℯ	σ	⊓	Prescription Secure Security
∂	∂ℯ	⊓	Inscribe-d Inscription Insecurity

F-HOOK.

⌐	⌐	⌐	Poverty [to have Perform-ed, Hope Performance
⌐	⌐	⌐	Develope-d Deform-ed-ity Difficult-y
⌐	ℓ	⁓	Advice, Advise-d Objective-ly Govern-ed
⁓	⁄	⁊	Government Refer Referred

N-HOOK.

⌐	⌐	⌐	Pennsylvania Punish-ed-ment Combine
⌐	⌐	⌐	Combined Combination Bank
⌐		⌐	Banker Bankable Bankrupt
⌐	∂		Bankruptcy At once But once
∂	∂	∫	Contention Tension Denominate-d

			Denomination
			Condensation
			Religion
			General-ly
			Imagine-ary, June
			Generalize
			Generalized
			Generalization
			Generation
			Gentlemen
			Gentleman
			Imagined
			Connect-ed
			Connection
			Continue-d
			Continual-ly
			Continuous
			Continuously
			Continuation
			Constitute-d
			Constitution
			Constable
			Account
			Accountable-y
			Begin, Organ
			Begun, Again
			Began
			Beginner
			Organize
			Organized
			Organic [graphy
			Forgotten, Phono-
			Financial-ly
			Within
			With interest
			Reference
			Men
			Man
			Human
			Meantime
			Women
			Woman
			Mental-ly
			Maintain
			Maintained
			Maintenance
			Any one, Opinion
			No one
			None
			Lengthen
			Uniform-ed-ity

Universe-al-ity
Behind
Behindhand

LARGE HOOKS.

Bewilder-ed
Dwell-ing, Dwelt
Quarter-ed

Question-ed
Acquiesce
Acquiesced

Acquisition
Quantity
Acquaint-ance

Railway
Familiar-ly-ity
Familiarize-d

Family
Themselves
Commission-ed

Commissioner
Memorandum
Memoranda

Minimum
Nominate-d
Nomination

TION-HOOK.

Occupation
Compassion
Passion

Opposition
Position
Possession

Attention
Decision
Situation

Objection
Justification
Accession

Accusation
Formation
Conviction

Recollection
Resolution
Examination

Institution
Information
Incision

RULES OF STENOTYPY.

A very convenient way of indicating stenographic forms, is by the use of Stenotypy, a method exhibited in the following rules and illustrations:

1. The stems Chay, Ith, The, Ish, Zhe and Ing, which cannot be represented in the English language by single letters, are indicated in Stenotypy by the Roman letters Ch, Th, Dh, Sh, Zh, and Ng, respectively. All other stems, except upstrokes, are indicated by Roman capitals.

2. The upstrokes Lay, Ray, and Shay, are indicated by the Italic letters *R, L* and *Sh*, respectively.

3. Small Roman letters (except g and h, used as above stated) indicate attachments to stems, such as circles, loops and hooks, and the sounds implied by the halving and lengthening principles.

4. The ticks, which are named, from the stems they resemble, the P-tick, T-tick, etc., are indicated by small Italic letters corresponding with such stems. The semi-circles are indicated by the small Italic letters *w* and *y*, and prefixes and affixes are also shown by small Italics.

5. A hyphen **shows** that the stems between which it occurs should be written very near each other, but unconnected.

6. A dot (·) indicates that the proper vowel should be inserted.

7. A cross (+) indicates that the stems should be intersected.

8. A superior figure indicates the position of the stem after which it is placed. Where no figure is given, the word should be written in the second position.

ILLUSTRATIONS OF STENOTYPY.

D¹		Psns		Pn		stT		Fltr	
K³		sPs		Pns		Tts		Fndr	
Ch		Pss		Pusn		Trt		*p* M³	
Sh		Psss		Pust		Tlt		*r* N	
Th		stP		Pnstr		Tut		*ch* M	
Dh		Pst		Tw		Tuts		*ch* w	
BKM		Pstr		Ty		Tft		Sh *p*	
RK		Pr		Ttr		Tfts		R *r*	
R K		Fr		Ttrs		sTrt		N *ch*	
LK		sPr		Ttrn		stRt		*w* D·	
L K		stPr		Tm		sTlt		*y* K	
FSh		Pl		Tms		stTt		Klu-L	
sP		sPl		Tmn		Ftr		com Bnsn¹	
Ps		Pf		Tt		Ftrs		RsP *ng*	
Psn		Pfs		sTt		Frthr		RsV + Dh	

CONTRACTIONS AND WORD-FORMS.

ALPHABETICALLY ARRANGED.

A

Abstract, Bs³Trt
Abstraction, Bs³Trsn
Accept, sPt³
Account, KNt³
Accustom, KsM³
Actionable-y, KsB³
Actual-ly, Kt²L
Actuality, KtLt³
Acknowledge, KJ
Acknowledged, KJd
Acknowledgement,
        [KJMnt
Acquaint-ance, Kwnt
Acquire, KwIt
Additional-ly, Ds³L
Adjourn-ed, Jr
Adjournment, JrMnt
Admeasure, DZhr
Administer, Ds³R
Administrate, Ds³Rt
Administration, Ds³Rsn
Administrative,
        [Ds³RtV
Administrator, Ds³Rtr
Administratrix, Ds³Ks
Adult, Dlt
Adulterous, DltRs
Advantageous, J³S
Advertise, Ts¹
Advertised, Tst¹
Advertisement, Ts¹Mnt
Advice, Advise-d, Dv³
Affect, Ft³
Affidavit, FtVt
Afflict, Flt³
Affliction, Flsn³
Again, Gn
Agency, JS
Agree, Gr¹
Agriculture-al, GrKl
Almighty God, bMtGd¹
Almost, Mst¹
Also, LS
Altogether, bG¹
American, MRKn or
        [MrKn
Amongst, Ngst
Angel, Jl
Anniversary, NV³

Antagonist, NtG³
Antedate, NtDt
Anticipate, NtsPt
Anticipation, NtsPsn
Antidote, NtDT
Anybody, NBd¹
Anyhow, Np¹
Any one, Nn¹
Any other, Nj¹
Anything, N¹Ng
Anyway, Nw¹
Apportion, P³Rsn
Appliance, Plns³
Applicable-ity, Pl³K
Applicant, Plnt³
Application, Plsn³
Apply, Pl³
Apprehend-ed, Prn³
Apprehension, Prnsn³
Apprehensive-ly, Prns³
Approve-al, Prv³
Architect-ure-al, R³K
Argue-ment, R³G
Arkansas, R³K
Arrangement, RMnt
As it-the, Zt³
As regards, Zrds³
Assemble-y, SM
Assignment, S¹Mnt
Assume, S³M
Assumption, S³Msn
Astonish-ment, St¹N
Astronomy-ical, St¹Rn
At all events, TlvNts
At any rate, TNrt
At last, TLst
At least, Tlst
At length, Tln
Atmosphere, TMsR
At once, Tns
Atonement, T'Mnt
Attainment, TMnt
Attention, Tsn
Attract, Trt³
Attraction, Trsn³
Attractive, Trv³
Auspicious, S¹P
Authentic-ity, Thnt¹
Authoritative-ly,
        [Thrt¹Tv
Authority, Thrt¹

Authorization, Thrssn¹
Authorize, Thrs¹
Authorized, Thrst¹
Averse, Vrs³
Aversion, Vrsn³
Avert, Vrt³
Awful, dFl¹
Awkward, KWrd¹

B

Balance, Blns³
Balanced, Blnst³
Bank, Bn³
Bankable, Bn³B
Banker, Bn³R
Bankrupt, Bn³Pt
Bankruptcy, Bn³S
Bank stock, Bs³K
Became, Become, BK
Because, Ks¹
Began, Gn³
Begin, Gn¹
Beginner, Gn¹R
Begun, Gn
Belief-ve-d, Bl
Belong-ed, Bl¹
Beneficent-ial-ly, BnF
Benevolent-ce, BNV
Bewilder-ed, Bw¹
Blank, Bln³
Bond and mortgage,
        [Bd¹MG
Bonds and mortgages,
        [Bds¹MGs
Bond and warrant,
        [Bnd¹Wnt
Bondholder, Bd¹Ldr
Bondsman, Bds¹Mn
Brother, Br³
Brother in law, Br³Nl
Brethren, Brn³
Built-d-ing, Bld¹
Business, Bss¹
But once, Tns³
By virtue of, B¹Vr

C

Calculate, Kl³Klt
Calculation, Kl³Klsn
California, KlF³

Capability, KBlt	Comprehensive-ly,	Cultivate, KltVt
Capable, KBl	[Prns[1]	Cultivation, KltVsn
Car, Kr[3]	Concern, sRn *or* sRn	Cure, Kr[3]
Care, Kr	Conclude, Kld[3]	Custom, Ksm
Cared, Krd	Concourse, KKrs[1]	Customer-ary, KsMR
Card, Carred, Krd[3]	Condensation, Dnssn	[*or* KsRt
Casual-ly, KZh	Conditional-ly, Ds[1]L	
Casualty, KZhT	Connect, Kn	**D**
Category-ical-ly, Kt[3]Gr	Connecticut, KNtKt	
Catholic, KTh	Connection, Kusn	Dark, During, Dr[3]
Cattle, KtL	Consequence, sKns[1]	Darken, Drn[3]
Caught, Kt[1]	Consequent, sKnt[1]	Darkens, Darkness,
Certain, sRtN *or* sRt	Consequential, sKn[1]	[Drns[3]
Certificate, sRtF	Consider-able-y, sDr	Danger, DJr
Certification, sRtFsn	Consideration, sDrsn	Dangerous, DJrs
Certif. of stock, sRtFst	Considerate, sDRt	Day or two, Drt
Certify, sRtF	Considered, sDrd	Dear, Dr[1]
Cemetery, sMtR	Consist, ssT[1]	Declaration, DKlsn
Challenge-d, Chl[3]	Consistence, ssTns	Declare, DKl
Charter-ed, Chtr[3]	Consistency, ssTn	Declarative, DKltV
Chattel mortgage-d,	Consistent, ssTnt[1]	Decree, Kr[1]
[Cht[3]MG	Constituency, stTn[1]	Decreed, Krd[1]
Child, Chilled, Chld[1]	Constituent, stTnt[1]	Dedicate, DDKt
Children, Chl	Construct, sTrt	Dedication, DDKsn
Character, KrK	Construction, sTrsn	Deduct, DdKt
Characteristic, KrKsK	Constructive, sTrv	Deduction, DdKsn
Characterize, KrKs	Constable, Knst	Deform-ed-ity, Df[1]
Characterized, KrKst	Constitute-ed, Knst[1]	Degree, Gr[1]
Charity, Chrt[3]	Constitution, Knstn[1]	Delaware, DlWr
Chemical-ly, KM	Continual-ly, KnL[1]	Deleterious, Dlt[1]Rs
Christian-ity, KrsCh	Continuation, Knsn[1]	Delight, Dlt[1]
Circulate, sRKlt	Continue, Kn[1]	Delinquent, Dln[1]
Circumference, sRns	Continues-ous, Kns[1]	Deliver-ed, Dl
Circumstance, sTns	Continuously, KnsL[1]	Deliverance, Dlns
Circumstantial-ly, sTn	Contingent-ly-cy, TnJ	Democrat-ic-y, DM
Citizen, sTzn[1]	Contract, Trt[1]	Demonstrate, DMnsTt
Claim-ed, Kl	Contraction, Trsn[1]	Demonstration,
Clerk, Kl[3]	Contradistinction,	[DMnsTtsn
Collateral-ly, KltRl[3]	[DstNg[1]	Demonstrative,
Collect, KlK[1]	Contradistinguish-ed,	[DMnsTv
Collection, KlKsn[1]	[Dst[1]	Denominate-d, Dn[1]
Collector, KlKtr[1]	Controversy, TrVr	Denomination, Dnsn[1]
Collective-ly, KlKv[1]	Conversation, Vrssn	Derivation, Drvsn[1]
Combination, Bnsn[1]	Converse, Vrs	Derive, Drv[1]
Combine, Bn[1]	Conversed, Vrst	Derived, Drvd[1]
Combined, Bnd[1]	Conversion, Vrsn	Describe-d, sKr[1]
Commercial-ly, KMr[1]	Convert, Vrt	Description, sKrsn[1]
Commission-ed, Km[1]	Convict, Vt[1]	Descriptive, sKrv[1]
Commissioner, KmR[1]	Conviction, Vsn[1]	Designate-d, DsG
Common law, KL[1]	Correct, Kr[1]K	Destitution, Dstn
Commonly, KL	Correction, Kr[1]Ksn	Destruction, DsTrsn
Comparison, P[3]Rsn	Corrective, Kr[1]Kv	Destructive, DsTrv
Compassion, Psn	Corrector, Kr[1]Ktr	Detach, DtCh
Compel, Pl	Could, Kd	Detail, Dt[1]L
Compensation, Pnssn	Could not, KdNt	Detect, Dt[1]Kt
Complaint-ed, Plnt	Could not tell, KdNtL	Detection, Dt[1]Ksn
Completion, Plsn[1]	Counsel-cil, Kns[3]L	Detective, DtKtV
Compliance, Plns[1]	Court, Krt	Determination, DTrnsn
Complication, Plsn	Crime, Krm[1]	Determine, DTrn
Comply, Pl[1]	Criminal-ly-ity, Krmn[1]	Determined, DTrnd
Comprehend-ed, Prn[1]	Crimination, Krmsn[1]	Develope, DvP
Comprehension, Prnsn[1]	Cross examination,	Devolve-d, D[1]Vl
b	[Krssn[1]	Difficult-y, Df
		Dignify-ty-ied, DG

Diligent-ly, DlJnt
Direct, Drt
Direct examination,
          [DrtsMsn
Direction, Drsn
Directly, DrtL
Disadvantage, DsJ
Discharge-d, DsCh
Disclaim-ed, DsKl
Discover-ed-y, DsK
Discriminate-d, DsKm
Discrimination,
          [DsKmsn
Distinct-ly, DstNgt
Distinguish-ed, Dst
District, DsTrt
District Att'y, DsTrN
District of Columbia,
Divine-ity, Vn¹   [DsKl
Doctor, Dr
Doctrine, D¹Trn
Domestic, DMsK
Doubtful, Dt³Fl
Downright, D³Rt
Down stairs, Dnstrs³
Downward, D³Wrd
Drank, Drn³
Drink, Drn¹
Drunk, Drn
Due, Dy
Duration, Drsn³
During, Dark, Dr³
Dwell-t-ing, Dw

E

Early, RL
East and west, St¹Wst
Easterly, St¹L
Eastern, St¹Rn
Editor, DtR
Effect, Ft
Efficiency, FsNS
Efficient, FsNt
Either one, Dhrn¹
Either way, Dhrw¹
Electric-al, LK
Electricity, LKsT
Emphatic-ally, MFt
Endeavor-ed, NDv
Engage-d, NG
England, Ng¹Lnd
English, NglSh
Enlarge, NJ³
Enlarged, N³Jd
Entire, Ntlt
Envelope, NVP
Episcopal, PsK
Equal-ly, Kl¹
Equalization, Klssn¹
Equalize, Kls¹
Equalized, Klst¹
Especial-ly, SP

Essential-ly, SN
Establish-ed, StB
Establishment, StBMnt
Esteem, St¹M
Eternal-ly-ity, Trn
Every, Vr
Everybody, VrBd
Every one, Vrn
Everything, VrNg
Everywhere, VrR
Evidence, Vd or VdNs
Exaggerate, sJrt
Exaggeration, sJrsn
Examination, sMsn³
Examine, sMn³
Examined, sMnd³
Except, sPt
Exception, sPsn
Exchange-d, KsCh
Exclaim, sKl
Exclamation, sKlMsn
Exclamatory, sKlMtR
Executor-y, GsR
Executrix, GsKs
Exhibit, sRt¹
Expand, sPnd³
Expanse-ive-ly, sPns³
Expansion, sPnsn³
Expect-d, sP³
Expectation, sPsn³
Expend-iture, KsPnd
Expense-ive-ly, sPns
Experience, sPrns¹
Experienced, sPrnst¹
Experiment-ed, sPr
Explain, sPln
Explained, sPlnd
Explanation, sPlnsn
Express, sPrs
Expressed, sPrst
Expression, sPrsn
Expressive, sPrsV
External-ly, sTr
Extinguish-ed, KsTNg
Extra, sTr³
Extract, sTrt³
Extraction, sTrsn³
Extraordinary-ily,
          [Kstr¹
Extravagant-ly, sTrv³
Extreme-ly, sTr¹
Extrinsic, sTrn¹

F

Fact, Ft³
Familiar-ly-ity, Fm
Familiarize-d, Fms
Family, Fm³
Farther, Fthr
Fashionable-y, Fs³B
Favorable-y, FvB
February, FB

Few, Fy³
Financial-ly, FnN
Foreman, FrMu
Forever, Fv
Forgive, FG
Forgiven, FGn
Forgotten, Fn
Formal-ly, F¹ML
Formation, Fsn¹
Former, F¹Mr
Formerly, F¹Rl
Fortunate, FRtNt
Fraud, Frd¹
Freedom, Frd¹M
Frequency, Frn¹
Frequent-ly, Frnt¹
Fugitive, F³Jt
Furnish-ed, Frn
Furniture, FrntR
Further, Frthr

G

Garden, GrdN
General-ly-ity, Jn
Generalization, Jnssn
Generalize, Jns
Generalized, Just
Generation, Jnsn
Gentle, JNtL
Gentleman, Jnt
Gentlemen, Jnt¹
Good deal, Gd²L
Good while, Gd²L
Govern-ed, Gv
Governor, GvR
Government, GvMnt
Grand, Grnd³
Grand jury, GrdJ³
Grant, GrNt³
Graduate, GrdT³
Graduation, GrdShn³
Gratitude, Grt³Td
Great Britain, GrtBrt
Great Brit. and Ireland,
          [GrtBrtRlnd
Great deal, Grt²L
Great while, Greatly,
          [Grt²L
Guardian, GrDn³
Guilt-y, Glt¹

H

Habit, Bt³
Habitual-ly, Bt³L
Harvest, R³Vst
Has it-the, Zt³
Health-y, LTh
He did not, Hd¹Nt
He had not, Hd²Nt
Henceforth, NsF
Heretofore, Rt¹Fr
Hesitate, ZTt

c

Hesitation, ZTsn
History, St¹R
Horticulture, Rt¹Kltr
Hospital, S¹PtL
Human, Mn³

I

Idaho, D¹H
Imagine-ary, Jn³
Imagination, Jnsn³
Imaginative, Jnt³V
   [or Jn³Tv
Imagined, Jnd³
Immediate-ly, M¹Mt
Impart, MPrt³
Impel, MPl
Impelled, MPld
Imperfect, MPrf¹
Imperfection, MPrfsn¹
Import-ant, MPrt¹
Importance, Imports,
   [MPrts¹
Improvement,
   [MPr³Mnt
In accordance with,
   [N¹KrdNs
In all respects, NlsPs
Inasmuch, NsCh³
Inconsiderable-y, nsDr
Inconsiderate, NsDRt
Inconsideration,nsDrsn
Inconsistent, NssTnt¹
Independent, NdPnd
Indifferent-ce, NDf¹
Indian Territory,
   [NdTRt
Indignation, NdGnsn¹
Indignant, NdG¹
Indiscriminate, NDsKm
Indispensible-y,
   [NdsPns
Individual-ly, NdVd¹
Inexperience, nsPrns¹
Inexperienced,nsPrnst¹
Inference, NFRns
Inferential-ly, NFRn
Influence, Ns¹
Influenced, Nst¹
Influences, Nss¹
Influential-ly, NShl¹
Inform-ed, NF
Informal-ly, NF¹ML
Information, NFsn or
Inhabit, NBt³   [Nsn¹
In order to, Nrdr¹
Inquire-y, NKr¹
Inquired, NKrd¹
In reference to, NrF
In regard to, Nrd¹
In relation to, Nrsn¹
In respect of, NrsPf
In respect to, NrsP
d

Inscribe, nsKr¹
Inscription, nsKrsn¹
Insecure, nsKr³
Insecurity, nsKrT³
Insignificance, NsGns¹
Insignificant, NsG¹
Insist, NssT¹
Insomuch, NSMCh
Instead, NsTd
Institute, NsTt.¹
Institution, Nstn¹
Instruct-ed, nsTr
Instruction, nsTrsn
Instructive, nsTrv
Instrument-al-ly,
   [nsTrMnt
Intelligence, NtJns
Intelligent, NtJnt
Interest, NtsT
Interested, NtsTt¹
Internal-ly, Tr¹
Interrogatory, NtG¹
Intersect, NtsKt
Intoxicate, NtKs¹
Intoxicated, NtKsTd¹
Intoxication, NtKssn¹
Intrinsic, NTrn¹
Invitation, NVtsn¹
Involve-d, NV¹
Involution, NVsn¹
Irreligious. Rr¹Js
Is it-the, Zt¹
Island, pLnd¹

J

January, JN
Joint stock company,
   [Jts¹KK
Judicatory, JdKTr
Judicature, JdKtr
Judicial-ly, JdShl
Judicious, JdSh
June, Jn³
Junior, Jury, Jr³
Jurisdiction, JrsDsn
Jurisprudence, JrsP
Justice of the Peace,
Justification, Jsn [JsP
Juvenile, Jv³

K

Kentucky, KntK
Knowledge, NJ

L

Landlord, Lnd³Rd
Largely, Jl³
Larger, Jr³
Largest, Jst³
Last week, Ls³K
Lastly, Ls³L

Lateral, Lt³Rl
Lawyer, Lr¹
Learn, Lrn
Learned, Lrnd
Learnéd, LrNd
Legislate-d-or-ure, LJ
Legislation, LJsn
Lengthen, Ngn
Lengthwise, Ng²Ws
Liberty, Br¹
Literal-ly, Lt¹Rl
Literature, LtRtr
Literary, LtRR
Longer, Ngr¹
Longest, Ngst¹

M

Majesty-ic, MJ³
Malformation, MlFsn³
Massachusetts, MsCh
Material-ly, MtRl
Mature   Mt³R
Man, Mn
Manner, Nr
Manufactory, MNFt
Manufacture-d, MNF
Manufacturer, MNFR
Manuscript, MsKPt
Meantime, MnM¹
Measure, Zhr
Measured, Zhrd
Mechanic-al, MKn
Melancholy, MLn
Member, Br
Memoranda, Mm²D
Memorandum, Mm
Men, Mn¹
Mental-ly, Mnt
Mention, Msn
Mentioned, Msnd
Mercantile, MrL
Merchandise, MrChs
Merchant, MrCh
Mere, Mr¹
Messenger, MsJr
Methodism, MsM¹
Metropolitan, MtRP
Mexico, MsK
Michigan, MSh
Microscope, MsKP
Minister-try, MnsT
Ministrate, MnsTt¹
Minimum, Mm¹
Misdemeanor, MsD
Misses, Mss¹
Mistake, MsK
Mistaken, MsKn
Mistook, Ms³K
Monstrous, MsTs¹
Montana, MntN¹
Mortgage-d, MrG¹
Movement, M³Mnt

Much more, Ch³M
Mutual-ly, MtL³
Mr., Mstr¹ or Mr¹
Mrs., MsZ or Mrs¹

N

Natural-ly, NtRl³
Naturalist-ized, NtRlst³
Naturalization, NtRlsn³
Naturalize, NtRls³
Near, Nor, Nr¹
Necessitate, NssTt
Neglect-ed, Glt
Negligence, Glns
Negligent-ly, Glnt
Negotiate, NGst
Negotiated, NGsTt
Neighborhood, NBrd
Neutral-ly, N·tRl³
Never, NV
Nevertheless, NVtLs
New Hampshire,
   [NMShr³
New Jersey, NJZ
New Mexico, NMsK
New Orleans, NRlns³
New York, NY
Next, Nst
Next day, Ns²D
Next month, Ns²Th
Next time, Ns²M
Next week, Ns²K
Next year, Ns²Y
Nominate-d, Nm¹
Nomination, Nmsn¹
Nobody, NBd
None, N·n
No one, Nn
No other, Nj [NrsTh
North and South,
North Carolina, NrKrL
North Dakota, NrDK
Northerly, NrthrL
Northern, NrDhn
Notify, NtF¹
Notwithstanding,
   [NtsTnd¹
November, NV
Now, Np

O

Objection, Jsn¹
Objectionable-y, Js¹B
Objective-ly, Jv¹
Obligation, Blsn¹
Observance, BsRns
Observation, BsRsn
Observe-d, BsR
Obstruct, BsTrt
Obstruction, BsTrsn
Occupancy, Pn¹S

Occupant, Put¹
Occupation, Psn¹
Occupied, Pd¹
October, KtBr
Occurrence, Krns
Once more, WsM
Once or twice, WsTs
One or two, Wrt
On either hand, Dhrnd¹
On one hand, chWnd
On the other hand,
   [Dhrnd
Operation, P¹Rsn
Opportunity, Prt
Opposition, Pssn¹
Ordinary, Rd¹Nr
Organ, Gn¹
Organic, GnK¹
Organization, Gnssn¹
Organize, Gns¹
Organized, Gnst¹
Organizer, Gn¹slt
Organism, GsM¹
Original-ly-ate-d, RJ
Ornament-ed-al,
   [Rn¹Mnt
Other one, Dhrn
Other way, Dhrw ·
Otherwise, Dhrs¹
Over, Vr¹

P

Parallel, P³RlL
Paralysis, P³Rlss
Paralyze, P³Rls
Particular-ly-ity, Prt¹
Passenger, PsJr
Passion, Psn³
Pasture, Pstr³
Patent, Pt³
Patentee, Pt³T
Patent right, Pt³Rt
Peculiar-ly-ity, PK
Pecuniary-ily, P³Kn
Penetrate, Pnt
Pennsylvania, Pn
Pension, Pnsn
People, Pl
Perfect-ly, Prf¹
Perfected, Prf¹Kt
Perfection, Prfsn¹
Perform-ed, Pf
Performance, PfNs
Performer, PfR
Perhaps, PrPs
Perpendicular-ly-ity,
Person, Prsn [PRP
Personal-ly, PrsL
Perspective, PrsP
Perspicuous, PRsP
Pertinent, PRtNnt
Philadelphia, FldF

Physician and surgeon,
Plaintiff, Plnt¹ [FssJn
Pleasure, Zhr³
Plenty, Plnt ·
Politic, Plt¹K
Political, Plt¹Kl
Politician, Plt¹Shn
Popular-ly-ity, PP
Portable, PRtBl
Portion, PRsn
Position, Pssn
Positively, Pst¹
Possess, Pss³
Possession, Pssn³
Possessor, Pss³R
Possible-y-ity, Ps¹
Postage, PsJ
Post mortem, PsM
Poverty, Pv¹
Practicable-ity,
   [Pr³KtBl
Practical-ly, Pr³Kt
Practice, Pr³
Practiced, Prst³
Prejudice-d, PrJ
Preliminary-ily, Pr¹Lm
Prepare, PrPr
Preponderance, PrnNs
Preponderate-d, Prn
Prescribe-d, sKr
Prescription, sKrsn
Prescriptive, sKrv
Preservation, PrsRsn
Preservative, PrsRtV
Preserve, PrsR
Pretty, Prt
Principle-al-ly, Prn
Privilege, PrvJ
Probable-y-ity, PrB
Production, PrDsn
Productive, PrDv
Professor, Prf¹
Proficient-ly-cy, PrfSh
Profit, Prft¹
Profitable-y, Prft¹B
Promulgate, PrMGt
Proof, Prf
Proper, Pr¹
Properly, Pr¹L
Propose, PrPs
Propriety, Pr¹Prt
Proud, Prd³
Prove, Prv
Providence, Dns³
Provident, Dnt³
Providential, Dn³
Public-ly, PB
Publication, PBsn
Publish-ed, PB
Punish-ed-ment, Pn³
Purpose, PRPs or Pr
Put forth, Pf³
Put off, P³F

              e

Q

Qualification, KlFsn
Qualify, KlF
Quality, KlT
Quarter, Kw[1]
Quantitative, Kwnt[1]V
Quantity, Kwnt[1]
Question, Kw
Quite, Kt[1]

R

Rail, Roll, Rl
Railroad, Rr
Railroad accident,
         [RrsDnt
Railroad stock, RrsK
Railway, Rw
Railway stock, RwsK
Real estate, RlsTt
Realization, Rlssn[1]
Realize, Rls[1]
Realized, Rlst[1]
Reality, RlT
Realty, RlT[1]
Reason, Rsn[1]
Reasonable-y, Rs[1]B
Recollection, Rsn
Recoverable, R[3]Bl
Refer, Rf
Referred, Rfd
Reference, Rns
Reform, RF
Reformation, RFsn
Regeneration, RJnsn
Regular-ly-ate-d, RG
Regulation, RGlsn
Relate, Rolled, Rld
Relation, Rlsn
Release, RLs
Released, RLst
Relevancy, RlVn
Reliance, Rlns[1]
Relied Rld[1]
Religion, Jn[1]
Religious, Js[1]
Relinquish-ed, Rln[1]
Rely, Rl[1]
Remain, RMn
Remark, Mr[1]
Remarkable-y, MrBl
Remarked, Mrt[1]
Remembrance, Brns
Represent-ed, Rl[1]
Representation, RPsn
Representative, RPv
Republican, RPBn
Republic-lish-ed, RPB
Repugnancy, RPG
Require, RKr
Required, RKrd
Reservation, RsRsn
f

Reserve-d, Rslt
Resignation, RsG
Resolution, Rssn[3]
Respect-ed, RsP
Respect've-ly, RsPv
Respectful-ly, RsPFl
Responsible-y-ity,
         [RsPns
Retrospect, RtRsP
Return, RtRn
Revelation, RVsn
Revenue, Reverend,
         [RV
Revolve-d-er, RV[1]
Rhode Island, RDLnd
Right angle, RtGl[1]
Roman Catholic, RKTh
Rule, Rl[3]
Ruled, Rld[3]

S

San Francisco, sNssK
Satisfaction, sTssn[3]
Satisfactorily, sTs[3]L
Satisfactory, sTs[3]R
Satisfies, sTss[3]
Satisfy-ied, sTs[3]
Saturday, sTRD
Secure, sKr[3]
September, sPtM
Serve, sRv
Set, sT
Set forth, sTf
Set off, sTt[1]
Settle, StL or sTl
Several, sV
Sight, sT[1]
Signature, sG[1]
Significance, sGns[1]
Signification, sGnsn[1]
Significant, sGnt[1]
Signify, sG[1]
Similar-ity, sM[1]
Similarly, sML
Single-ular-ly-ity, sNg[1]
Singly, sNgL
Sister in law, SstrnL[1]
Situate, sCh[1]
Situation, sChsn[1]
Somebody, sM[2]Bd
Something, sMNg
Sometime, sMm
Somewhat, sMt[1]
Sought, sT[1]
South Carolina, sKrLN
South Dakota, sDK
Southeastern, sTbstrn[3]
Southerly, SthrL
Southern, sDhn
Southwestern, sWstrn[3]
Speak, Speech, sP[1]
Speaker, sP[1]R

Special-ly, sP
Spirit, sPrt[1]
Spiritual-ly, sPrt[1]L
Spiritualism, sPrt[1]LsM
Spoke, sP
Spoken, sPn
Spontaneous-ly, sPnt[1]
Startle, stltt[3]L
Stockbroker, stKBr
Stockholder, stKLdr
Stranger, sTrJr
Strength, sTr
Subdivide, sBdVd
Subdivision, sBdVsn
Subject, sB
Subjected, sBd
Subjection, sBsn
Subjective-ly, sBv
Sufficiency, sFsNS
Sufficient, sFsNt
Suggest-ed-ion, sJ
Suggestive, sJv
Suit, sT[3]
Summon, Some one,
         [sMn
Subordinate, sBr[1]
Subordination, sBrsn[1]
Subpoena-ed, sB
Subscribe-d-r, sB[1]
Subscription, Sbsn[1]
Substantial-ly, sBsTn
Substitute, sBsTt
Substitution, sBstn
Superficial-ly, sPrfSh[3]
Superintend-ent,
         [sPrntNd
Superstructure, sPrsTr
Suppress, sPrs[3]
Suppression, sPrsn[3]
Supreme, sPr[1]
Surprise, sPrs[1]
Swear, sW[3]
Swore, sW
Sworn, sWn
Sympathize, sMThs
Sympathy, sMTh
Synonymous, sNn[1]
System, ssT

T

Technical-ly, TK
Telegraph-ic, TlGr
Telegram, TlGrm
Telephone, TLFn
Temper, TPr
Temperance, TPrns
Temperate, TPrt
Temperature, TPrtr
Tennessee, TnS
Testament, TsMnt
Testify, TsF
Testimony, TsMN

Tension, Tnsn
Thenceforth, DhsF
Theoretical, Th*Rt*K1
Therefor-fore, *R*F
These, Dhs[1]
This, Dhs
Those, Dhs[3]
Thousand, Ths[3]
Throttle, Thrt[1]L
Thursday, ThrsD
Thwart, Th[1]Wrt
Timber, TBr
Timely, ML
Title, T[1]Tl
Today, *p*[2]D
Tomorrow, *pMR*
Torment, Tr[1]Mnt
Torn, Turn, T*R*n
Torpor, Tr[1]Pr
Tort, T[1]*R*t
Tolerate, Tl[1]*R*t
Total, TTl
Toward, Trd
Township, Tns[3]Sh
Townsman, Ts[3]Mn
Tract, Trt
Trade, Trd
Trade-mark, TrdM
Tradesman, TrdsMn
Transaction, Trnssn[3]
Transatlantic, TrsLntK
Transcript, TrsKPt
Transition, Trnssn[1]
Transfer-red, TrsF
Transform-ed, Trs[1]F
Translation, Trs*L*sn
Transparent, Trs[3]Pt
Transplant, Trs[3]Plnt
Transverse, Trs[3]Vrs
Treasurer, Trs*R*
Treasury, Trs*R*
Trustworthy, TrsDh
True, Tr[3]
Truth, Tr
Truthful, Trf
Typewriter, T*R*tr
Typewriting, T*R*tN*g*

U

Ultimate, LtMt
Unanimous, YnNMs
Unconsidered, nsDrd
Undergo, NdG
Understand, NdsTnd
Understood, NdsTd
Undertake, NdK
Undertaken, NdKn
Undertook, NdT[3]
Uniform-ed-ly-ity, Union, Yn[3]N   [Yn[3]F
United States, Yss[3]
Universe-al-ly, Yn[3]V
University, Yn[3]VsT
Unless, N1s
Until, NtL
Unusual-ly, NZh
Up stairs, Pstrs
Utah, *y*T[3]

V

Value, Vl[3]
Vanish, Vn[3]*Sh*
Variation, V*R*sn
Various, Verse, V*R*s
Verdict, Vrd
Versed, V*R*st
Version, V*R*sn
Very, Vr
Vicissitude, Vss[1]Td
Vindication, VndKsn[1]
Vindictive, Vnd[1]Kt*V*
Vitiate, V[1]Sht
Vocabulary, VKBl*R*
Voluntary, Vln[1]
Vulgar, VlGr

W

Wages, *w*Js
Walk, *w*K[1]
Wanton, Wnt[1]N
Was it-the, Zt
Wealth-y, W1
Weekly, *w*K1[1]

Welcome, WlK
Westerly, Ws*L*
Western, Wstrn
Westward, WsWd
Wharf, W*R*f
Whatever, Tf[1]
Whereabout, R[3]Bt
Whereas, Rs[3]
Wherefore, RFr
Wisdom, Zd[1]M
Withdraw, Dh[1]Dr
Withhold, Dh[1]Ld
Within, Dhn[1]
With interest, Dhnt[1]
Without interest, Wnt[1]
Without regard to, [Wrd[1]
Without relation to, [Wrsn[1]
With reference to, [Dhrf[1] *or* Dhr[1]F
With regard to, Dhrd[1]
With relation to, [Dhrsn[1]
Withstand, Dhs[1]Tnd
Witness, Wt[1]Ns *or* Wt[1]
Woman, *w*Mn
Women, *w*Mn[1]
Word, Wrd
Work, Wr
Workman, WrMn
Workmanlike, WrLK
Workmanship, World, *R*ld   [WrMnSh
Worship, Wr*Sh*
Worthless, Th*L*s
Written, *R*t[1]N

Y

Yearly, Y[1]L
Year or two, Yrt[1]
Yesterday, YstrD
Yes, sir, Yss
Yield, Yld[1]
Younger, Yr
Youngest, Yst
Youngster, Ystr

INITIALS.

In writing proper names, the consonant stems may be used for initials, except for C, Q and X, which may be indicated by the ordinary script letters, made very small. Gay should be used for both the whispered and vocal sounds of G. The vowels, when used for initials, are written as indicated below. It is unnecessary to place periods after initials, but it is well to underscore the whole name with a single straight line.

· A   · E   ᵛ I   ⸴ O   ⌃ U

SIMILAR WORDS DISTINGUISHED.

Apostle, Ps^{1}L
Epistle, Ps^{1}L
Postal, PsL

Patient, PShnt
Compassionate, PsNt
Passionate, Ps^{8}Nt

Opposition, Pssn^1
Position, Pssn
Possession, Pssn^8
Apposition, ·Pssn^8

Pertain, PRtN
Appertain, P^{8}RtN
Puritan, P^{8}RTn

Preparation, PrPrsn
Appropriation, Pr^{8}Prsn
Proportion, PrPRsn

Prediction, Prt^{1}Ksn
Protection, PrtKsn
Production, PrDsn
Predication, PrDKsn

Prosecute, Prs^{1}Kt
Persecute, PRsKt

·Prompt, Prmt^1
Permit, Pr^{1}Mt
Promote, PrMt

Proximate, Prs^{1}Mt
Approximate, Pr^{1}Ks

Prominent, Prm^{1}Nnt
Preëminent, Pr^{1}MnNt
Permanent, PrMNNt
Paramount, Pr^{8}Mnt

Spirit, sPrt^1
Separate, sPrt
Support, Sport, sPRt

Special-ly, sP
Especial-ly, SP

Beautify, Bt^{8}F
Beatify, BTF

Business, Bss^1
Baseness, BsNs
Absence, Bs^{8}Ns

Abundant, BndNt
Abandoned, Bn^{8}Dnd

Birth, BRTh
Breath, BrTh

Attainable, TnB
Tenable, TNBl

Contractor, Trt^{1}R
Trader, TrdR
Traitor, Trtr
Territory, TrtR

Train, Trn
Turn, TRn

Daughter, Dtr^1
Debtor, Dtr
Auditor, Dt^{1}R
Auditory, Dt^{1}R
Editor, DtR
Doubter, Dt^{8}R
Dietary, D^{1}TR

Dilation, D^{1}Lsn [DLsn
Delusion, Dilution,
Adulation, D^{8}Lsn

Deceased, DSst
Diseased, DsZd

Domination, Dm^{1}Nsn
Condemnation, DmNsn
Damnation, Dm^{8}Nsn
Diminution, D^{1}MNsn
Dimension, DMNsn
Admonition, DMnShn

Derision, Drsn^1
Direction, Drsn
Duration, Drsn^8
Adoration, D^{8}Rsn

Causation, Kssn^1
Accession, Kssn
Accusation, Kssn^8

Extension, sTnsn
Extenuation, sTnYsn

Collision, Klsn^1
Coalition, KLsn
Collusion, KLsn^8

Credence, KrDns
Accordance, Krt^{1}Ns

Garden, GrdN
Guardian, GrDn^8

Favored, FfRd
Favorite, FfRt

Physical, Fs^{1}Kl
Fiscal, Fs^{1}KL

Volition, V^{1}Lsn
Violation, VLsn
Evolution, V^{8}Lsn
Convulsion, Vlsn
Valuation, Vlsn^8

Voluble, Vl^{8}Bl
Valuable, Vl^{8}Rl
Available, VLBl

Vocation, VKsn
Avocation, V^{8}Ksn

Eastern, Historian,
Astern, StRn [St^{1}Rn
Stearine, stlRn^1
Stern, stRn
Con-strain, sTrn
Citron, sT^{1}Rn
Saturn, sT^{8}Rn

Altitude, LtTD
Latitude, Lt^{8}Td

Alcohol, LKL
Alkali, LKL

Writer, Rtr^1
Reader, RDr
Orator, Rt^{1}R
Oratory, Rt^{1}R
Oratorio, Rt^{8}R·
Rioter, R^{1}TR

Radiant, RDnt
Ardent, R^{8}Dnt
Hardened, chRd^{8}Nd

In fact, N^{1}Ft
In effect, NFt

Indication, Nd^{1}Ksn
Induction, NDsn
Intoxication, Nt^{1}Kssn

Invasion, NVsn
Innovation, NNVsn

Indicted, N^{1}Dtr
Indebted, NdTt
Undated, NDtr
Undoubted, N^{8}Dtr

Undefined, NDf^{1}Nd
Indefinite, NDfNt

Ingenious, NJNs
Ingenuous, NJNYs

Unavoidable, NVd^{1}Bl
Inevitable, NVTBl

64

POSITIVE AND NEGATIVE WORDS.

Advisable, Dv^3B
Inadvisable, NDv^3B

Appear, Pr^1
Disappear, Ds^1Pr

Artificial, Rt^2FsL
Inartificial, Nrt^2FsL

Balanced, $Blnst^3$
Unbalanced, $NBlnst^3$

Broken, $BrKn$
Unbroken, $NBrKn$

Ceremonious, $sRMNs$
Unceremonious,
[$nsRMNs$

Changeable, $ChBl$
Unchangeable, $NChBl$

Civil, sVl^1
Uncivil, $nsVl^1$

Comfort, Frt
Discomfort, Ds-Frt

Competent, P^1Tnt
Incompetent, N-Tnt

Complete, Plt^1
Incomplete, N-Plt^1

Conscious, Shs
Unconscious, N-Shs

Conceive, sV^1
Misconceive, Ms-sV^1

Connect, Kn^2
Disconnect, $DsKn^2$

Considered, $sDrd$
Unconsidered, $nsDrd$

Considerable, sDr
Inconsiderable, $nsDr$

Considerate, $sDRt$
Inconsiderate, $NsDRt$

Continue, Kn^1
Discontinue, Ds^1Kn

Consistent, $asTnt^1$
Inconsistent, $NssTnt^1$

Defined, Df^1Nd
Undefined, NDf^1Nd

Definite, $DfNt$
Indefinite, $NDfNt$

Determined, $DTrnd$
Undetermined, $NDTrnd$

Destructible, $DsTrtBl$
Indestructible,
[$NDsTrtBl$

Dignified, DG
Undignified, NDG

Efficient, $FsNt$
Inefficient, $NFsNt$

Elegant, $LGnt$
Inelegant, $NLGnt$

Glorious, Gls, or $GlRs$
Inglorious, $NGls$, or
[$NGlRs$

Important, $MPrt^1$
Unimportant, $NMPrt^1$

Legal, LGl
Illegal, $LlGl$

Legitimate, $LJtMt$
Illegitimate, $LlJtMt$

Liberal, $LBrL$
Illiberal, $LlBrL$

Logical, $LJKl$
Illogical, $LlJKl$

Material, $MtRl$
Immaterial, $MMtRl$

Mature, MtR^3
Immature, $MMtR^3$

Mortal, MRt^1L
Immortal, $MMRt^1L$

Noxious, $NKShs$
Innoxious, $NNKShs$

Numbered, Brd^3
Unnumbered, $NBrd^3$

Organic, GnK^1
Inorganic, $NGnK^1$

Organized, $Gnst^1$
Disorganized, Ds^1Gnst
Unorganized, $NGnst^1$

Partial, Pr^3Shl
Impartial, MPr^3Shl

Perfect, Prf^1
Imperfect, $MPrf^1$

Polite, P^1Lt
Impolite, MP^1Lt

Practicable, Pr^3KtBl
Impracticable,
[MPr^3KtBl

Proper, Pr^1
Improper, MPr^1

Profitable, $Prft^1B$
Unprofitable, $NPrft^1B$

Prudent, Pr^3Dnt
Imprudent, MPr^3Dnt

Pure, P^2R
Impure, MP^3R

Qualified, $KlFd^1$
Disqualified, Ds^1KlFd
Unqualified, $NKlFd^1$

Questioned, Kw
Unquestioned, NKw

Rational, $RsnL$
Irrational, RsL

Redeemed, R^1Dmd
Unredeemed, $NrDmd^1$

Reduced, R^3Dst
Unreduced, $NrDst^3$

Regular, RG
Irregular, RG

Relevant, $RlVnt$
Irrelevant, $RLVnt$

Respective, $RsPv$
Irrespective, $RsPv$

Responsible, $RsPns$
Irresponsible, $RsPns$

Resolute, $RsLt$
Irresolute, $RsLt$

Satisfied, sT_b^3
Dissatisfied, Dss^2Ts
Unsatisfied, $NsTs^3$

Significant, sG^1
Insignificant, NsG^1

Similar, sM^1
Dissimilar, Dss^1M

Solvent, sL^1Vnt
Insolvent, NsL^1Vnt

Spoken, sPn
Unspoken, $NsPn$

Sufficient, $sFsNt$
Insufficient, $NsFsNt$

Understood, $NdsTd$
Misunderstood,
[$MsNdsTd$

Variable, $VRBl$
Invariable, $NVRBl$

Washed, $wSht^1$
Unwashed, $NwSht^1$

Worthy, Dh
Unworthy, NDh

OUTLINES FOR IMPORTANT WORDS.

A. A, An, or And is indicated by a K-tick, lu phrasing. In a very few instances the T-tick is used where the K-tick will not make a distinct angle with the stem.

Abrupt-ness BRPt
Absolute BsLt 3
Abstinence BsTuNs
Absurd-ity BsRt 3
Abject BJt 3
Accessible-y-lty KssB 3
Accessory-ary KssR 3
Accident-al sDnt 3
Accordance KrdNs 1
Accredit KrDt 3
Accurate Krt 3
Accuracy KrS 3
Acquire Kwlt 1
Acquired Kwltd 1
Acquit Kwt 1
Acquittance KwtNs 1
Actuate KtT 3
Adequate DKwt 3
Admiralty DMRlt 3
Admit DMt
Admonish DMnSh
Advancement DsMnt 3
Adventure DvNtr
Adversity DVrsT 3
Advert DVrt 3
Advocate DvKt 3
Affirmative FrMtV 3
Affluence ·FlNs 3
Affluent ·FlNt 3
Afterward FWrd 3
Aggregate GrGT 3
Aggregation GrGsn
Agriculturist GrKlst
Alarm LRm 3
Alarmed Litmd 3
Aliment LMut 3
Alleviate LVt 1
Alleviation LVsn 1
Alliteration LtRsn 1
Alphabet LFBt
Although bDh
Altitude LtTD
Amanuensis-ses MnNss
Ambiguity MBG
Ameliorate MLRt 1
Ammunition MNsn3
Amusement MsMnt 3
Analogy NlJ 3
Anchor NgKr 3
Anger-y Ngr 3
Anguish NgSh 3
Annoyance NNs 1
Annual-ly NL 3
Anonymous NnMs 1
Antagonism NtGsM 3
Anterior NTRR 3
Antiquarian NtKwRn
Antique NtK 1
Antiquity NtKT
Anxiety NgsT
Anxious NgShs
Apartment PrtMnt 3
Aperture PRtr 3

Apparent PRnt
Appertain PRtN 3
Appointment PntMnti
Approbation PrBsn 3
Appreciate PrSht
Approach PrCh
Approximate PrKs[1]
Aptitude PtTt 3
Arbitrary RBtRR
Ardent RDnt 3
Aristocrat-cy RsTK
Arithmetic RThMt
Arrange RnJ
Arouse Rs 3
Article RtKl
Articulate RtKlt
Artificial-ly RtFsL
Ascend-t, Assent, Snt
Ascribe SKr
Ascription SKrsn
Aspect SPt 3
Aspersion SPrsn
Aspiration SPRsn
Assert Srt
Assert ion Srsn
Assiduity SDT
Assimilate SMLt
Assistance SsTns
Associate SSht
Association SShsn
Attendance TndNs
Audacious-ly DSh
Audacity DsT 3
Auditor DtR 1
Auditory DtR 1
Augment GMnt 1
Auxiliary KsLR
Available VLBl
Avaricious VrShs 3
Avenge VNJ
Average VrJ 3
Avocation VKsn 3
Avoid Vd 1
Avoidance VdNs 1
Awaken WKn
Aware WR

B. Baptist-ize BP
Baptism BPsM
Barbarity Br-B
Barbarous BRBrs 3
Barometer BrMtr
Beatify BTF
Beauteous BTS 3
Beautify BtF 3
Beautiful-ly BtFl 3
Behalf BF
Behave BVr
Behavior BVR
Benefaction BnFsn
Benefactor BnFtr
Benignant BNG
Bespeak BsP 1
Beware Bwlt
Bigot-ry BGt 1
Bill of sale BlsL 1
Biography-er BGr 1
Bishop-ric BSh 1
Birth BRTh
Board Brd
Board of trade BrdTrd
Bounty BnT 3

Bountiful-ly BntF 3
Breadth BrdTh
Breath BrTh
Brilliant BrLnt
Brilliancy BrLnS
Builder Bldlt
Burdensome BrdsM

C. Cabinet KB 3
Calculable KlBl 3
Call forth Klf 1
Campaign Kl'n
Candidate KndDt
Canonical KnNKl1
Capital-ly KPtL
Catalogue KtLG
Cautious KSbs 1
Capricious-ly KPrSh
Catholicism KThsM
Celebrate-ity sLBrt
Censure sNShr
Chaplain ChPln 3
Charitable-y Chrt
Chastity ChsTT
Cheerful-ly Chrf 1
Childhood ChldHd 1
Chimerical KmRKl
Christianize KrsChns
Circuit slcKt
Circular slcKlt
Circulation slcKlsn
Clear KlR 1
Coalition KLsn 1
Colonist KlNst 1
Colonization KlNssn 1
Colony KlN 1
Comfort Frt
Communicate NKt 3
Communication NKsn
Community Nt 3
Commonest Kst 1
Complimucut FlMnt
Complete Plt 1
Conceal sL 1
Concentrate sNTrt
Concession Knssn 1
Conciliate sLT 1
Condemnation
　　[DmNsn
Condensation Dnssu
Conformable-y
　　FrMBl 1
Congenial JNL 1
Congestion Jstn
Congratulate GrtLt3
Conjunction JNgsn 1
Conscience Shns
Conscientious ShNShs
Conscious bhs
Conservative sRVtV
Consist ssT 1
Consolation sLsn
Conspicuous sPK 1
Constant sTnt 1
Constitutional-ly
　　[KnstnL 1
Constitutionality
　　[KnstnLt 1
Consumption sMsn
Coutaminate TnnNt 3
Contend Tud 1
Contention Tnsn 1

Contrivance TrvNs 1
Control TrL
Conversant VrsNt
Co-opera'e Kl'Rt 1
Co-operation KPRssn 1
Cordial-ly KrDL
Corporeal KrPRl
Credeuce KrDns
Credulity KrDLT 3
Criticise KrtsZ
Criticism KrtssM
Culpable-y KlBl
Cupidity KPT
Curiosity KRsT 3
Curious KRs 3
Cursory KrsR

D. Damnation
　　[DmNsn 3
Daughter Dtr 1
Debenture DBnt
Deceptive DsPtV
Declaim DKIM
Declension DKlnsn
Declination DKlNsn
Debility D-B
Decease DSs 1
Defense DfNs
Deficiency DfSh
Degenerate DJn
Degeneration DJnsn
Degrade DGrd
Degradation DGrdsn
Deject DJt
Dejection DJsn
Deliberate DlBrt
Delicate DlKt
Delicacy DlKS
Delusion DLsn
Demoralization
　　[DMRlssn 1
Demoralize DMRls 1
Denounce DnNs
Denunciation
　　[DnNssn
Depart DPrt
Department DPrtMnt
Deponent DPNt
Depraved DPrvt
Depravity DPrvT
Deprecate DPrKt
Depreciate DPrSht
Derange DrNJ
Deride Drd 1
Derision Drsn 1
Derogate DrGt
Descend-t DsNt
Deserve DsR
Desideratum DsDrtM
Desire DsIt
Desolate DsLt
Desperate DsPrt
Desperation DsPrsn
Despicable-y DsP
Despond-ent-cy
　　[DsPnd 1
Despotism Dsl'tsM
Destructible DsTrtBl
Detestable-y DTst
Detract DTrt 3
Detraction DTrsn 3

66

Detriment-al DTrMnt	Entertainment [NtTMnt	Fertile FrtL	Hereditament [HrdMnt 1
Diametrical-ly [DMtKl 1	Entire NtR	Fertility FrtLt	Hereditary HrdR 1
Diction DKsn 1	Equator Kwtr	Fidelity F-D 1	Herewith ltr 1
Differential DFrn 1	Equatorial KwtRl	Final-ly FNl 1	Heroine chRn 1
Dilution DLsn	Equivalent KwV	Finality FNlt	Higher, Hi e chR 1
Diminish DMNSh	Error Rr	Finish FnSh	Highest chSt 1
Diminution DMNsn 1	Erroneous RrNs	Firm Frm	Highly chL 1
Diplomacy DPlMS	Escape SKP	Fiscal FsKL 1	Highway chW
Diplomat-ic DPlMt	Essence SNs	Flexible-y-ity FlKsB	Historian StRn 1
Director DrtR	Estimate 8tMt	Fluent FlNt	Hitherto DhrT 1
Disappoint-ment [DsPnt 1	Estimation StMsn	Foolish FLSh 3	Honestly NstL
Discontinue-d DsKn 1	Eulogy LJ 3	Foretell FTl	Horizontal-ly HRsNtL
Discontinuation [DsKnsn 1	Europe RP 3	Foretold FTld	Horticulturist [RtKlst 1
Discountenance [DsKntNns	European RPn 3	Foreign FRn	Hospitable-y SPtBl 1
Disease DsZ	Enthusiasm NThssM	Foreigner FRnR	Hospitality SPtLt 1
Discordant DsKrdNt 1	Enthusiast-ic NThssT	Forge-ry FrJ	Humanity MnT 3
Discreet DsKrt 1	Evangelical VNJ 3	For instance FsTns	Humor Mr 3
Discrepancy DsKrP	Evangelist VNJLst 3	Forsake FsK	Hunger-y Ngr
Dishonor DsNr 1	Evangelization [VNJLssn 3	Forthwith FRThw	Hypocrite PKrt 1
Disparage DsPRJ	Evaporate VPrt 3	Forward FWrd	Hypocrisy PKrS 1
Dispelled DsPLd	Eventual-ly VNtL	Foundation FndShn 3	
Dispensation DsPnssn	Eventuate VNtYt	Fountain FntN 3	
Dispersion DsPRsn	Everlasting VrLsNG	Faction FKan 3	**I.** At the beginning
Displayed DsPld	Exact GsKt, or sKt 3	Fractious-ly FrKShs	of a phrase, *I* is in-
Displeasure DaZhr	Exaction GsKsn, or [sKsn 3	Fragment-ary FrG 3	dicated by a P- or Ray-
Dis-re-member DsLr	Example GsMPl	Frantic FrntK 3	tick, except before Ar
Dissatisfy DssTs	Excellence KsLns	Fraternal-ly FrtrNl	or Way, when the T-
Dissatisfaction DssTsn	Excellency KsLnS	Fraternity FrtrNT	tick is used In the
Dissolution DsLsn 3	Exasperate GssPRt	Frigid-ity FrJd 1	middle or at the end
Distract DsTrt 3	Exceptionable-y sPsB	Froward FrWrd	of a phrase, *I* is indi-
Distraction DsTrsn 3	Exchequer KsChK	Frugal-ly FrGl 3	cated by the T-tick.
Distribute DsTrBt	Exclude sKld 3	Frugality FrGlt 3	
Diversity DVrsT	Exemplify GsMPlF	Fruition Frsn 3	Identical-ly rDtKl 1
Divest DVst	Exemplification [GsMPlFsn	Fundamental-ly [FndMnt	Identification [rDntFsn 1
Divination DvNsn 1	Explicit KsPlsT	Furious FRs 3	Idleness DlNs 1
Divulge DVlJ	Evolution VLsn 3	Futurity FTRt 3 or [F-T 3	Ignorance GNrns
Downcast DnKst 3	Exquisite KsKwsT		Illustrate LsTrt
Downhearted Dnlttr	Extemporaneous [KsTPrNs	**G.** Gallery GLr 3	Illustration LsTrsn
Downright DRt 3	Extemporary KsTPrR	Genial-ly JNL	Imaginable JnB 3
Dramatic DrltK	Extempore KsTPr	Genteel JNTL	Imbecile MBsL
Dyspepsia-tic DsPP	Extemporize KsTPrs	Gentle JNtL	Imbecility MBsLt
	Extensible sTnsB	Geometry JMtR	Immaterial-ly MMtKl
E. Earnest RNst	Exterior KsTRR	Glorify GlF	Immateriality MMtRlt
Eccentricity [KsNtrsT	Exterminate [KsTrmNt	Glorification GlFsn	Immature MItR 3
Ecclesiast-ic KlssT	Extinct KsNgt 1	Glorious Gls	Immaturity MMtRt 3
Economy KnM 1	Extinction KsNgsn	Glory Gl	Immigrate MMGrt 1
Education DKsn	Extract sTrt 3	Gracious GrShs	Immigration [MMGrsn 1
Effeminate FmNt	Extraction sTrsn 3	Gradual-ly GrDL 3	Imminent MMnNt 1
Efficacious-ly FKShs	Extremity sTrmT	Grandeur Grndlt3	Immoderate MMdRt 1
Elaborate LBrt 3	Eyesight 'St 1	Grateful-ly GrtFl	Immoral MMRl 1
Element LMnt		Gratify GrtF 3	Immorality MMRlt 1
Elevate LVt	**F.** Facetious-ly FsSh	Gratitude GrtTd 3	Immortal-ly MMtRtL 1
Elevation LVsn	Factious-ly [FKShs 3		Immortality [MMRtLt 1
Eloquence LKwns	Factitious-ly FKTSh	**H.** Habeas corpus [BsKr 3	Immutable-y MMtBl 3
Emblem MBlM	Failure FLR	Handsome NdsM 3	Imperceptible-y [MPrsPtBl
Emblematic MBlMt	Faintest FntSt	Harmonious RMNs	Impervious MPrVs
Emigrate MGrt	Fainthearted FntRtr		Implacable-y MPlKBl
Emigration MGrsn	Faithful-ly-ness FTbf	*HE*, at the beginning	Implicit MPlsT
Eminent MnNt	False Fls 1	of a phrase, is indi-	Impolitic MPltK 1
Empty MT	Falsify Fl-F 1	cated by the Chay-	Imposed MPsD
Endanger NDJr	Famish FmSh	tick; in the middle	Impost MPst
Endless NdLs 3	Fanciful-ly FNsF 3	or at the end of	Impoverish MPv 1
Energy NrJ	Fastidious FsTDs	a phrase, by a P-,	Impregnate MPrG
Energetic NrJtK	Fatality FtLt	Chay-, or Ray-tick,	Inartificial-ly NrtFsL
Engagement NGMnt	Fantastic-ally FNTstK	struck at a distinct	Inauspicious-ly NsPSh
Evening Vn 1	Favored FrRd	angle.	Incessant NssNt
Enormity NrMT	Favorite FvRt		Incivility nsVlT
Enormous NrMs 1	Female FML	Health LTh	Inclination NKlNsn 1
Enroll NRl		Heart chRt 3	Incombustible N-Bst
Entangle NtNgGl 3		Heathen Dhn 1	Incompetent N-Tnt 1
		Herald HRld	
		Herein RN 1	

Incompetence N-Tns
Inconstant N-sTnt 1
Incredible-y [NKrdBl
Incredulity NKrdLt 1
Indebted NdTd
Indeed NDd 1
Indefatigable-ity [NdFtBl 3
Indefinite NDfNt
Indemnity-fy NDm
Indemnification [NDmFsn
Indenture NdNtr
Indescribable NdsKBl
Indication NdKsn
Indict NDt 1
Indicted NDtr 1
Indictment NDtMnt 1
Indiscreet NDsKrt 1
Indisposition NDsPssn
Individuible-y NdVsBl
Indulge NdLJ
Inevitable-y NVTBl
Infection NFKsn
Inference NFRns
Inferential-ly NFRn
Inferior NFRr
Inferiority NFRr
Inferred NFRd
Infidel NFdL
Infidelity NFdLt
Infinitude NFNTd
Infirm-ity NFrm
Informal NFML
Informality NFMLt 1
Infraction NFrKsn 3
Infringe NFrNJ
Ingenious NJNs
Ingenuity NJNT
Ingenuous NJNYs
Ingredient NGrDnt 1
Initial-ly NShl 1
Inherit Nrt 1
Inheritance NrtNs 1
Injure-y NJr
Innocence NsNs 1
Innovation NNVsn
Insert NsRt
In so far as NSFs
Insolence nsLns 1
Inspection NsPKsn
Inspiration nsPrsn 1
Inspire nsPr 1
Instant-ly NsTnt 1
Instinct-ive-ly NsNgrt 1
Insufferable-y NsFBl
Insufficient NsFaNt
Insulation nsLsn
Insult nsLt 1
Insuperable-y [nsPrBl 3
Integrity NtGrT
Intellect-ual-ly NtLt 1
Intelligible-y NtLBl
Intemperance NTPrns
Intemperate NTPrt
Intention NtNsn
Interception NtrsPsn
Intercession Ntrssn 1
Interchange NtrCh
Interior NTRR
International [NtrNsnL
Interpret NtrPrt

Interpretation [NtrPrtsn
Intervention NtVNsn
Intestate NTsTt
Intimate Ntilt 1
Intimidate NTmDt
Intolerable-y NtLrBl
Introduce NtDs
Introduction NtDsn
Introspection NtsPKsn
Intuition NTsn 3
Invention NVnsn
Investigate NVsGt
Investigation NVsGsn
Invisible-y NVsBl
Invitation NVtsn 1
Inward NWrd 1
Iron Rn 1
Ironical-ly RnK 1
Irrecoverable-y Rr 3
Irresistible-y RssT
Itself TsLf

IT, when the last word of a phrase and preceded by a half-length stem, is indicated by a P-, Ray-, or Chay-tick, struck at a distinct angle with the half-length or with its final hook.

J. Jehovah JV
Jesus JsS
Joint committee JtK 1
Judiciary JdShR 3
Justice JsTs
Juxtaposition JsPssn

L. Lament LMnt
Latitudinarian [LtTdNrn £
Legal-ly LGl
Legality LGlt
Lexicographer-y [LKsK
Limit LMt
Limitation LMtsn
Luxuriance LKsRns
Luxuriant LKsRnt
Luxury LKsR

M. Magnanimous-ly [MGNn
Magnet-ic MGNt
Magnetism MGsm
Majority MJrt 1
Malicious-ly MLSh 2
Malignant MlG 1
Mansion MNsn
Mature MtR 3
Medical-ly MdKl
Med. treatment [MdTrtMnt
Medicine Mdsn
Medium MdM 1
Merciful-ly MRsF
Metaphor-ical-ly MtFr
Method MThd
Migrate MGrt 1
Migration MGrsn 1
Ministration MnsTsn 2
Miracle MRKl
Misrepresented MsRP

Misrepresentation [MsRPsn
Mission MShn 1
Missionary MShR 1
Mistrust-ful MsTrsFl
Mitigate MtGt I
Mitigation MtGsn 1
Modification MdFsn
Modify MdF
Murder MRdr
Murderous MRdrs
Mutable-y MtBl 3
Mystery MsTR
Mysterious MsTRs
Mystify MsT 1
Mystification MstFsn 1

N. Narrate NRrt 3
Narration [NRrsn 3
Narrative NRrtV 3
Navigate NVG 3
Navigation NVGsn 3
Necessarily NssKl
Needful NdF 1
Needle NDl 1
Needless NdLs 1
Negative NGtV
Nomenclature Nmn
Nondescript [NNdsKPt 1
Notification NtFsn
Nourish NrSh
Noxious NKShs

O. Obedience BDns
Obscure BsKr 3
Obscurity BsKrt 3
Observatory BsRvtR
Obsolete BsLt 1
Official-ly FShl 1
Officious-ly FShs 1
Oftentimes FnMs 1
Ofttimes FtMs 1
Oligarchy LGrK
Omnific MNFK 1
Omniscient MNsNt 1
Omnipotent MNP 1
Omnipresent MPrsNt 1
Only Nl
Onward rWrd 1
Opposite PsT
Orthodox-y RThD
Ostentatious-ly [StNtShs 1
Outcast TKst 3
Outward TWrd 3
Overwhelm VrLm 1
Overwhelmed [VrLmd 1

P. Paganism PGsM
Painful PnF
Paragraph PrGrf 3
Parliament-ary [PrLMnt 3
Partial-ly-ity PrShl 3
Partake PRtK 3
Particle PRtKl 3
Partner PrtNr 3
Patentable PtBl 3
Paternity PtRNT
Patriarch PtRK
Patron PTrn 3
Pattern PtRn 3
Peevish-ly PvSh 1

Penalty PNlT
Penitent PnTnt
Penitential-ly PnTn
Penitentiary PnTnSh
Per annum PRNm
Per cent. PRsNt
Perishable-y PRShB
Permanence PrMNNs
Permit PrMt 1
Pernicious-ly PrNSh
Perpetual-ly PRPt
Persecute PRsKt
Perseverance [PrsVRns
Persevere PrsVR
Personality-ity PrsNlT
Personify PrsNF
Personification [PrsNFsn
Persuade PrsWd
Persuasion PrsWsn
Pertinacious-ly [PRtNSh
Pestilence PsTLns
Pestilential PsTLn
Petrify PtRF 2
Phenomena FNm
Phenomenon FNmn
Photograph-er-ic [FtGrf
Physical-ly FsKl 1
Physiognomy FsG 1
Piquant PKnt 1
Piquancy PKnS 1
Platform PltF
Plentiful-ly PlntF
Plenipotentiary PlnP
Plural PLRl
Plurality PlRlt
Polygamy PlGM 1
Ponderous PndRs
Pontiff PntF 1
Posterior PsTRR
Potential-ly PTnSh
Posterity Ps-T
Practiced Prst 3
Previous PrVs
Precipitate PrsPTt
Precisely PrssL 1
Precision Prssn 1
Predestinate PrDstNt
Predestination [PrDstNsn
Predominance PrDm
Predominant [PrDmNnt
Pre-eminent PrMnNt 1
Prejudicial-ly PrJd
Prerogative PrRG
Presentation PrsNtsn
Preserved PrsR
Preservation PrsRsn
Preservative PrsRtV
Presbyterian PrsBt
Presidential PrsDn
Pretense PrTns
Pretension PrTnsn
Prevent PrvNt
Prevention PrvNsn
Priestcraft PrsKft 1
Prima facie PrmSh
Probation PrBsn
Problematic-al PrBl
Proclaim PrKl
Proclamation PrKlsn

Prodigal PrdGl 1	Rejection RJKsn	Scepticism sKPtsM
Prodigious PrdJs 1	Relent Klnt	Scholar sKLr 1
Proficient-ly-cy PrfSh	Relevancy KlVn	School sKl 3
Prognosticate-d PrG 1	Relevant KlVnt	Scientific SNtF 1
Prohibition PrBsn 1	Reliable-y KlBl 1	Scoundrel-ly sKndKL
Prominent PrmNnt 1	Reliability RlBlt 1	Scrutiny sKrtN 3
Promulgation	Itelish KlSh	Scripture sKr 1
[PrMGsn	Relnctant-ce KlKtNs	Scriptural sKrL 1
Pronounce PrnNs	Remittance RMt 1	Season Ssn 1
Pronunciation	Remonstrance	Seasonable-y 8sB 1
[PrnXssn	[RMnsTns	Seclude sKld 3
Prophetic PrftK 1	Remonstrate RMnsTt	Seclusion sKlsn 3
Propitious PrPSh	Render KndR	Secretary sKrtK
Prosecute PrsKt	Renounce RnNs 3	Sec. of the Navy
Proscription PrsKrsn	Renunciation	[sKrtNV
Proscriptive PrsKrtV	[RPrn	Sec. of State sKrtsTt
Prospect PrsPt 1	Repetition KPtsn 1	Sec. of War sKrtWr
Prospective-ly PrsPv 1	Repentance RPntNs	Sectarian sKTKn
Prosperity PrsPrt 1	Replenish-ed KPln	Secular sKlK
Prostitute-d PrsTt 1	Reprehensible-y-ity	Sedentary sDntR
Protect PrtKt	[KPrn	Sedition sDsn 1
Protection PrtKsn	Reprehensive KPrns	Seize sZ 1
Protestant PrtsTnt 1	Reproach KPrCh	Seldom sLdM
Protract PrTrt	Reputation KPtsn 3	Senator sNtr
Protraction PrTrsn	Resemble-ed-ance RsM	Senior sNR
Provincial PrvNSh	Reserve-d RsR	Sensual-ly-ity sNShl
Prudential-ly PrDn	Resplendent-ly	Sentence sNtNs
Pugnacious-ly	[RsPlnd	Sentiment-al-ly
[PGNShs	Respond-ent RsPnd	[sNtMnt
Pugnacity PGNsT	Responsible-ity RsPns	Sequence sKwns 1
Pulpit PLPt	Restore RsTR	Servile sRVL
Punctual-ly PNgL	Restoration KsTRsn	Servility sRVLt
Punctuality PNgLt	Restrict RsTrt 1	Short sighted
Pusillanimous-ly	Restriction RsTrsn 1	[ShrtsTd 1
[PsLnMs	Restrictive KsTrf 1	Simplicity sMPlsT
	Resurrection RsKsn	Simplification
Q. Qualitative KltTv	Retort RTRt	Sister Sstr 1 [sMPlFsn
Questionable-y	Retract KTrt 3	Skill sKl 1
[KwBl	Retraction RTrsn 3	Slander sLndr
Questioner KwK	Retreat RTrt 1	Slanderous sLndrs
Quick KK 1	Retrospection	Slumber sLmR
Quiet KwT	[RtRsPsn	Smaller sMLR 1
	Retrospective RtRsPv	Social-ly sShl
R. Radiant RDnt	Return RtRn	Socialism sShlsM
R. R. station	Returnable-y RtRnB	So far as 8Fs
[RrsTsn	Reveal RVL	Solitary sLtR 1
R. W. station RwsTsn	Revenge RVNJ	Solvency sLVn 1
Ramification RMFsn	Revengeful-ly RVNJf	Solvent sLVnt 1
Rapacious RPShs	Revert RVKt	Spacious sPShs
Rapid-ity KPd 3	Reversion RVKsn	Speakable sPBl 1
Rascal RsKL 3	Revive RVv 1	Specialty sPShlt
Ratification RtFsn 3	Revivify KVF 1	Specify-ic sPsF
Ratify KtF 3	Revolt RVLt	Specification sPsFsn
Recapitulate KKPt	Reward RWrd	Species sPShs 1
Recipient RsPnt 1	Rhetoric RtRK	Speculate sPKlt
Reciprocate RsP 1	Rhetorical-ly RtRKl	Spendthrift sPndThft
Reclaim RKlM	Righteous RChs 1	Splendid sPlnDd
Reclamation RKlMsn	Romance RMns	Splendor sPlndr
Recognition R-Nsn	Romantic RMntK	Spontaneous sPntNs1
Recognize R-Ns	Romanism RMsM	Square sKwR
Recommendation	Runaway RnW	Standard sTndRd
[R-Ndsn		Statesman stTsMn
Record RKrd	**S.** Sacred sKrd	Statistics stTstKs
Redeem KDm 1	Sadden sDn 3	Stereotype stRtP 1
Redemption RdMsn	Sadness sDNs 3	Strange sTrNJ
Reduction KDsn	Sanctification	Strengthen sTrNgThn
Redundant-ly-cy	[sNgtFsn 3	Structure sTrtr
[RDndNt	Sanctify sNgtF 3	Stupendous stPnDs
Reflection KFlKsn	Sanction sNgsn 3	Stupidity stPdT
Reflective KFlKv	Sanctioned sNgsnd 3	Subjugate sBJGt
Reformatory RFtr 1	Sanctity sNgtT 3	Sublime-ity sBlM
Refraction KFrKsn 3	Sanguine sNGwn	Subordinate sBr 1
Refractory KFrK 3	Saviour sVR	Subordination
Reiterate R TRt 1	Scale sKL	[sBrnsn 1
Reject RJt	Sceptic sKPt	Subsequent-ly sBsKnt

Subserve sBaR
Subservient sBaRVnt
Substantiate-d
[sBsTnSht
Substantive sBsTntV
Substantial-ly sBsTn
Substitute sBsTt
Subtract sBTrt 3
Subtraction sBTrsn 3
Succinct sKsNgt 1
Suffocate sFKT
Suffocation sFKsn
Summer-ary sMR
Superficial-ly sPrfSh 3
Superincumbent
[sPrn-Bnt 3
Superinduce sPrnDs 3
Superiority sPRr
Superlative-ly sPrLtV
Supernatural-ly
[sP-NtRl 3
Superscription
[sPrsKsn 3
Superstition sPrsTsn 3
Supplicate sPlKt
Supplication sPlKsn
Support sPRt
Supreme Court sPrKrt 1
Surrender sRndR
Surreptitious-ly
[sRPtsSh
Surround sRnd 3
Surveyed sRVd
Survive sRVv
Survivor sRVvR
Suspect-ed ssP
Suspend ssPnd
Suspense ssPns
Suspension ssPnsn
Suspicion ssPsn
Sustain ssTn
Sustenance ssTnNs
Sustentation ssTntShn
Swindle-r sWnd 1
Sympathetic sMTht
Systematic ssTMt
T. Tabernacle
[TBrNKl
Taciturn-ity TrtKn
Tangible-y TnJ
Tantamount TntMnt 3
Temperament TPrMnt
Temporal-ly TPrL
Temporality TPrLt
Temporary TPrR
Tempt TMt
Temptation TMtsn
Tenable TNBl
Tendency TndNS
Tenement TnMnt
Terminate TrmNt
Termination TrmNsn
Testamentary TsMntR
Testimonial TsMNL
Texture TKstr
Thankful-ly Thf 3
Thankworthy ThDh 3
THE is indicated, at the beginning of a phrase, by the Chay- or Ray-tick; in the middle of a phrase by the P-, Chay-, or Ray-tick.

Thereto *Rp*	Unavoidable-y [NVdBl 1	Utterly *TrL*	**W.** Wander Wndr
Theretofore RtF	Uncertain NsRtN		Want Wnt 1
Thermometer ThrMm	Unclaimed NKl 2	**V.** Vacancy VKnS	Warehouse WrS
Third Thrd	Uncommon NK 1	Vacant VKNt	Warm wRm
Thousandth ThsTh 3	Undefined NDfNd 1	Valedictory VlDtR	Warmed wRmd 1
Throughout ThrT 3	Unexceptionable-y [NsPsB	Valid-ity VLd 3	Warrant WRnt
Timid-ity TMd 1	Undergone NdGn	Valuable VlBl 3	Water works WtWs 1
Tolerance TlRns 1	Underhanded [NdrNdch	Valuation Vlsn 3	Wayward WWrd
Tolerant TlRnt 1	Unequivocal-ly NKwV	Value Vl 3	Whatsoever TsV 1
Torpid TrPd 1	Unexpected-ly NsP 3	Vanish VnSh 3	Whence Hs
Trader TrdR	Unfortunate NFRtNt	Venality VNlT 3	Whenever Hv
Tragedy TrJ 3	Unimagined NJnd 3	Vengeance VNJns	Whensoever HsV
Traitor Trtr	Unparalleled [NPRlLd 3	Veracious VrShs	Wherein RN 2
Tranquil-ly TrNKl	Unpopular-ly-ity NPP	Veracity VrsT 3	Whereof Rf 1
Tranquility TrNKlt	Unquestioned NKw	Veterinary VtrNr	Wheresoever RsV
Transcendent [TrsNdNt 3	Unreasonable-y [NrsB	Vexatious-ly VKShs	Wherever Rv
Transcribe TrsKli 3	Unreliable-y-ity [NRlBl 1	Vice president [VPsDnt	Wherewith Rw
Transgress TrsGs 3	Unruly NRl 3	Vice versa VsV 1	Whilst Lst 1
Transgression [TrsGsn 3	Unsatisfactory [NsTsR 3	Vicious VShs 1	Whither chWtr
Transient TrnShnt	Unscriptural nsKrL	Violation VLsn	Wholesale LsL 3
Transparent TrsPRnt	Unsecured nsKrd 3	Violent VLnt	Whomsoever MsV 3
Treachery TrChr	Unselfish nsLfSh	Virtual-ly VrtL	Whosoever fsV
Tuition Tsn 3	Unspeakable-y NsPB11	Virtuous VrChs	Wicked WKd 1 or [wKd 1
Turn TRn	Unwilling NLNg	Visible-y VrBl	Willingly LNgL
Typograph-er-ic TPGr	Upward PWrd	Visionary VsnR 1	Withstand DhsTnd 1
		Vitality VtLt 1	Withstood DhsTd 1
U. Ultimatum [LtMtM]		Viva voce VV 1	Wretched RChd
Unaccepted NsPt 3		Vocation VKsn	
		Volition VLsn 1	**Z.** Zeal ZL 1
		Voracious VRShs	Zealous ZLs
		Voter Vtr	Zest Zst

THE CHOICE OF OUTLINES.

In the foregoing lists, the student is furnished with nearly four thousand useful outlines. Of these, the word-signs and contractions should be perfectly memorized. The other outlines given are not only valuable for reference as to the correct forms to be used for the particular words contained in the lists, but they are suggestive of the best outlines for a vast number of other words which the stenographer will be likely to meet in his work. The flexibility of this system of writing is such, that words may often be written in two or more different ways, either of which is legible. For example, the word *calendar* may be written with either of the following outlines:

The choice of the best outline for a word, often requires careful thought, but when the question is once decided, the same form should always be used for that word. To use different forms for the same word, is sure to cause hesitation and loss of speed. In such words as fall under the rule at section 25, *b*, examples of which are given on page 64, great care should be taken to select distinct and unambiguous outlines. Most of the words in the English language which come under this rule, are contained in the Phonetic Shorthand Word-Book, with engraved forms for the same, and every stenographer should possess a copy of that book.

TABLE OF CONTRASTS.

See Key, next page.

71

Diagram of Vowels.—This diagram should be carefully compared with the rules contained in section 4, *d*, on page 8, which give directions for the placing of vowels between two stems. In such cases, the vowels which appear at the left of the diagonal line in the diagram, are written *after the first stem ;* and those appearing at the right of that line are written *before the second stém.*

At several points in the Writing Exercises, reference is made to lines in the Table of Contrasts, page 71. Wherever such reference is made, the examples referred to should be carefully read and compared with each other. A key to these examples is given below :

LINE 1.   Sip, Spa.   Sight, Sty.   Opes, Pose.   Oppose.   Suppose.

2.   Ask, Sack.   Asp, Sap.   Acid, Sad.   Assail, Sail.   Escape, Scape.

3.   Puss, Pussy.   Daze, Daisy.   Gas, Gassy.   Fuss, Fussy. Moss, Mossy.

4.   Back, Bask.   Tuck, Tusk.   Deck, Desk.   Tack, Task.   Gap, Gasp.   Rap, Rasp.

5.   Czar, Sir.   Zeal, Seal.   Zero, Sorry.   Zinc, Sink.   Dozen, Design.   Reason, Resign.

6.   Pace, Paces.   Toss, Tosses.   Chase, Chases.   Case, Cases. Face, Faces.   Vice, Vices.   Lace, Laces.   Mosses.

7.   Policy, Policies.   Intimacy, Intimacies.   Ecstasy, Ecstasies. Posy, Posies.   Fancy, Fancies.   Daisies.

8.   Chess, Chest, Chester.   Less, Lest, Lester.   State, Taste. Steel, Least.   Stop, Post.   Posts, Posten, Posten's.

9.   Pray, Play.   Breach, Bleach.   Eager, Glee.   Free, Flee. Ether, Ethel.   Error, Earl.   Eater, Tree.   Eagle, Glee.

10.   Sup, Supper, Supple.   Set, Setter, Settle.   Side, Cider, Sidle.   Sick, Sicker, Sickle.   Scape, Scrape.   Sorrel.

11.   Stop, Stopper.   Stout, Stouter.   Staid, Staider.   Stitch, Stitcher.   Stalk, Stalker.   Stag, Stagger.   Safe, Safer, Civil.

12.   Poison, Poisoner.   Paster, Pastry.   Besiege, Besieger. Duster, Destroy. Disguise, Disgrace.   Dispose, Displays.   Disobey, Disables.

13.   Pen, Penny.   Tine, Tiny.   Dean, Deny.   Chine, China. Gain, Guinea.   Fin, Finny.   Mince.

14.   Pays, Pains.   Days, Danes.   Chase, Chains.   Skies, Skins, Screens.   Boughs, Bounce, Bounced.   Punsters.

15.   Pun, Puff.   Bean, Beef.   Tun, Tough.   Chain, Chafe. Cane, Cave.   Fine, Fife.   Lean, Leaf   Knife.

16.   Puff, Puffy.   Beef, Bevy.   Tough, Taffy.   Dave, Davy. Chafe, Chaffee.   Cough, Coffee.   Gravy.

17.   Past, Pats, Pants.   Best, Beds, Bends.   Toast, Totes, Tends. Chest, Cheats, Chants.   Cost, Cuts, Counts.   Base, Banes.

WRITING EXERCISES.

The exercises which appear in the following pages, illustrate every principle of Phonetic Shorthand. Practice should be confined to these exercises, until all the rules of abbreviation are learned. No attempt should be made to write miscellaneous matter, for the reason that such matter is likely to contain many words which can only be written correctly under rules which appear later in the study. Writing such words incorrectly, will lead the student into bad habits of writing which it will be difficult to overcome.

Before attempting to write an exercise, the rule under which it is to be written should be carefully read, together with such additional suggestions as appear in connection with the exercise. Each form should be written with care, and no exercise should be left until the student can not only write it readily and correctly, but read it *aloud*, without hesitation, from his own manuscript.

Sec. 4. a, b. Long Vowels are indicated by heavy dots and dashes. Write the following words in the positions required by subdivision *b*. Rules 1, 2, and 3, refer to the positions of *upright and inclined stems only*—not to those of horizontal stems. When R or L is printed in Italic, use the upward stem, and remember that first-place vowels are placed at the *beginning* of a stem, whether the stem be struck upward or downward.

/ Paw, pea, pooh, pa, pay, ape, ope. Be, bay, bah, bo. Abe. Tea, tay, toe, too. Eat, ate, ought, oat. Day, daw, doe, Dee. Aid, awed, ode. Chaw, each. Gee, jay, jaw, joe, age. Key, caw, coe, coo. Eke, ache, oak. Gay, go. Oaf, eve. Oath, thaw. They, though. See, say, saw, so. Ease, awes, owes, ooze. *Le, lay, la, law, low, loo.* Eel, ai*l,* aw*l,* O*la.* · *Ray, raw, roe.* Ear, air, oar. Me, may, ma, maw. Aim. Knee, nay, gnaw, no. E'en, own. We, way, wah, wo, woo. Ye, yea, you. He, hay, hah, haw, hoe, who.

c. Short Vowels are indicated by light dots and dashes. When a vowel occurs between two stems, place it as directed in subd. *d*. Remember to write all words in their proper positions, as directed in subd. *b*.

Υ Up, pugh, at, add, odd, etch, edge, egg, off, if, us. Pot, pet, pat, pod. Bit, bet, bat, bog, bug, bag. Tick, tuck, tack, took, tag, tip, top, tap. Ditch, dig, dip, dutch, duck, dumb, dam. Chip, chap, chub, chid, chuck, chick. Jim, gem, jam, jug, jag, Gyp, jab. Kip, cop, cod, kedge, cup, cab, cub, cad, catch, cuff, cough, king. Got, giddy, gap. Fib, Fitch, fob, fetch, fudge, funny, Fanny, fatty, finny, fag. Vim, Vick. Thick, thud, thatch, thumb. Ship, shop, shove, sham, shad. Minnie, money, mob, much, match, Maggie. Not, nit, gnat, nut, nip, nap, nob, nab, nub, knack, knock, nook, notch, nag, nudge.

The following exercise contains both long and short vowels. Place each word in its proper position, and do not forget to write the vowels as directed in subd. *d.* Make the proper distinction between long and short vowels, but do not make the former too heavy. (*See diagram of vowels, page 71.*)

Peat, paid, pot, pet, pat, pod. Beat, bait, bet, bat, bought, boat, boot. Teak, talk, took, tick, tuck, tack. Deem, dome, dumb, doom. Check, chair, choke, chip, chap. Jeer, joke, jug, jag. Cape, cup, calm, caulk, comb, cage, kedge, cab, bog, balm, cod, cuff, keel, coal, core. Gear, game, gawk, gig, gage, gap. Reap, rake, rock, root, rag, rub. Feat, fade, food, fib, fun, fan, fudge, fag. Vat, vote, veto, veal, valley. Evade, evoke. Thebe, thought, theme, Thane, them, thumb, thole, thatch, thick, thill. Sheet, shade, shape, shiny, shame, sham, shoot, assure. Leap, lobe, lake, lap, leash Meed, made, mar, Maud, mode, meadow, mood, month, mate. Neat, nail, node, nudge, nib, not, note, nut, kneel, nag, natty, uneasy.

e. Diphthongs.—The signs for the diphthongs must not be inclined. When I occurs between two stems, it is sometimes more convenient to write it in the third place, rather than to carry the pen back to the beginning of the first stem. Do not forget that when the position of an outline depends upon this diphthong, it is always to be considered as first-place.

Pie, pew. By, boy, bough. Tie, toy. Die, dow, dew. Chow, chew. Joy, Jew. Coy, cow, cue. Guy. Fie, few. Vie, vow, view. Thigh, thew. Thy, thou. Sigh, soy, sue. Shy. Lie, lieu, alloy, allow. Rye, Roy, row, rue. My, mow, mew. Nigh, annoy, now, new. Bite. Boyd, bowed, beauty. Dyke, dime, dowdy, duke. Chide, chewed. Jibe, jewed. Kite, coif, cowed, cube. Fido, fire, fiery, feud. Vied, vowed, void, viewed. Shire, shower. Mike, mouth, mule. Knife, noisy, newt.

f. A vowel after a diphthong, is indicated by an inclined tick Make the angles distinct.

Piety, pious, bias, Diana, diet, Zion, scion, boyish, voyage, dewy, annuity, fewer, viewer, bowing.

g. Write the following words and indicate the vowels by the inclined angle, as directed in the rule. Be careful to shade the down-stroke of the angle, when the first vowel is long. In using this angle, the student will notice that the exact quality of the second vowel is not indicated. This will not cause any difficulty in reading, however, as the word can be distinguished readily by giving that vowel the sound of Ĭ, or ŭ.

Poet, poesy, Bowen, being, bayer, toeing, jawing, Boaz, chaos, thawy, showy, piano, *r*uin.

h. Iota, idea, *R*hea, panacea, iambic. Bough, eyed, oily, *r*ye, vow, view, few.

j. Always join the semi-circle to a stem at a distinct angle. Two forms are given, for the purpose of making this possible Make the semi-circles small. If made too large, they will appear awkward, and will be mistaken for half-length stems.

Weep, web, Utah, Yattau, Yedo, Utica, widow, watch, witch, yoke, wake, wick, waggish, Oswego, youth, wash, y*ell*ow, Eu*r*ope, U*r*ania, yam, wing, young.

Sec. 5. Rules for L, R, and Sh.—The rules in this section are very important. Do not leave them until you can write every word correctly in the following exercise. The legibility of your writing will be much greater, if you learn to apply these rules correctly and readily.

The use of Italics to indicate upstrokes, will be continued in the following exercises in exceptional cases only.*

*L*aw, elk, delay, array, parry, shade, bush. Lieu, alum, dally, airy, aurora, ship, fish. Lay, alimony, pulley, Arab, foray, pshaw, share, bushy, low. Alumni. jolly, ray, bar, show, coolie, ark, worry, shame. Fishy, eel, Electa, valley, leach, army, veil, roe, marry, loo, sheaf, show, dashy.

Awl, latch, Allegany, pillow, pill, rue, tire, shore, dash, aisle. Leap, pile, lobe, isle, cheer, shoe, cash. Bailey, oily, lip, fowl, rubbish, far, ask, ash, laugh, allow. Mash, anneal, dual, leash.

Albany, meal, aright, peer, opera, chair, reel, early, share, folio, elbow, mill, arrayed, peal, pour, rally, mole. Feel, ivory, elfish, mall, urge, mellow, pale, moor, aerial, rehash. Alvah, mail, earth, tare, olive, belay, apiary, ball. Bear, berry, awry, toil, tar, billow, shape, burrow, bole. Bureau, shake, follow, Romish, tyro, dole, bellow, dower, fair. Tarry, allege, remedy, Howell, cherry, also, rely.

*Extensive lists of words ending with L and R will be found on pages 92 and 93.

Sec. 6. Heath, hail, heap, highway, happy, hymn. Halve, heal, humbug, hurl, whip. Unhook, half, huzzy, hammock, hawk. Had, hug, home, whey, hash, hallow. Hope, higher, hoggish, whack, whew, hook. Whim, harmony, hob, hair, hoop. Hop, whir, wherry, hilly, whirligig.

Sec. 7. **Word=Signs.**—Learn the word-signs thoroughly. Then carefully read the sentences on page 13, and copy them in shorthand and read them from your own writing. It will be much better if you can read your exercises aloud. Practice faithfully, until you can both read and write them correctly and without hesitation. Then translate the following sentences into shorthand, and practice upon them in the same way. Use word-signs for all words printed in Italic, vocalizing the other outlines. If you practice in this manner, you will be surprised at the progress you will make.

1. Show *it to him, before you put it away.* 2. *That was what was given to* her. 3. *If she can go, it will* be *as well.* 4. *Do what you can for* me. 5. *Shall I take it to the* shop? 6. *There was* no *change when he was there.* 7. *Did they hear from you when you were away?* 8. *He and I were there at the* time. 9. *They took it out in a* pail. 10. *I wish she would come with him, too.* 11. *They live there, and have come here for the* fair. 12. *Who was on the* boat? 13. *It was too high for him.* 14. *We ought to do all we can.* 15. *Why did you give our* book *to him?* 16. *They each had a watch which was given by him.* 17. *He came an hour before he should have come.* 18. *Two of their* sheep *were in the* road. 19. *Has he as* many *as you or I have?* 20. *Did they give you any of their* candy?

a. Read the rule very carefully. Then write the following phrases, joining the words which are connected by hyphens, and placing the first word of each phrase in its proper position. All these phrases are composed of word-signs contained in the list on page 13.

That-was. What-was. If-she-can. You-can. There-was. He-was. She-would. Who-was. It-was. We-can. Which-was. Did-they. Give-that. Before-that. She-can. Shall-come. Can-they. Or-that. Can-do. Was-that. That-they. She-came-in.

b. **Ticks.**—It is very important that the pupil make no mistake in the use of the ticks. If the wrong tick is used for a word, it will naturally be read for a different word, and the proper sense of the phrase or sentence will be destroyed.

INITIAL TICKS ON SIMPLE STEMS.

HE.—When a phrase begins with *He*, always use the Chay-tick, (⁄) except before Lay, where a T-tick (ı) is used. *He* cannot be indicated by a joined tick before either of the stems | | ⁄ ⁄ ∟ ∟ ((⌣ ⌣ ×

I.—*I* is indicated by the T-tick (ı) before ⌐ and ⌐ ; by the P-tick (＼) before ⌐ ⁄ ⌒ ⌒ ; and by the Ray-tick (‑) before any other stem.

THE.—*The* is indicated by the T-tick (ı) before ⌐ ; by the Chay-tick (⁄) before — —)) ⌡ ⌡ ⌐ ⌒ · ⌐ ⌒ ⁄ ; and by the Ray-tick before any other stem.

A, AN, AND.—Use the T-tick (ı) before — —)) ⌐ ⌐ ⌐ × Use the K-tick (‑) before any other stem.

MEDIAL TICKS.

In the middle of a phrase, either *He* or *The* may be indicated by the P-, Ray-, or Chay-tick, but no tick is to be used where it will not make a distinct angle with the stems.

I is never written in the middle of a phrase, except by the T-tick.

A, An, and *And*, are indicated by a K- or T-tick, in the middle of a phrase.

FINAL TICKS.

He and *The* are indicated by a P-, Ray-, or Chay-tick, at the end of a phrase.

A, An, and *And*, are indicated by a K- or T-tick, at the end of a phrase.

I is indicated finally, by the T-tick only.

☞ Observe carefully the direction given in subd. *c*. When a phrase begins with either of the ticks for the words above mentioned, the second word of the phrase is placed in the position directed in § 4, *b*, and not the tick. Make the ticks exactly one-fourth the length of a stem.

Read and copy the first eleven lines on page 15, and carefully note the application of the above rules.

Sec. 8. S-Circle.—Don't make a loop for a circle. A loop is not a circle, but means something entirely different. On a straight stem, turn a simple circle with a motion opposite that of the hands of a watch, except in a few instances where it occurs between stems. A circle between a tick and a stem, is written as if it were between two stems. (*See lines 1 to 5, Table of Contrasts, p. 71.*)

Sip, sup, sap, peace, pus, pass, sob. Boys, seat, sight, sty, stow, seedy, said, such, sage. seek, sky, spy, spa, tease, dose, chase, joss. Safe, suffice, face, phiz, suffuse, save, salve, vice, voice, views, saith, sooth, thaws, seethe, scythe. Cease, seize, sighs, size, says, saws, sues, sash, ashes, seem, same, psalm, mace, moss, muss, mice, mouse, muse, moose. Seen, sane, sawn, soon, sin, son, sign, niece, nose, news, sing, sung, sang, song. Wise, ways, wooes, use, hawse, lies, hues. Speedy, speech, spoke, subdue, Sabbath, stake, scope, scathe. Scotch, sigma, sphere, safety, civic, savage, savings, snob, snipe, snatch, snore. Snug, smack, smoky, small, singing, swap, swab, swing, swag.

c. Asp, espy, osage, ask, Ezra, Isaac, assume, oozing, assignee. Esty, easier, asthma. Saucy, busy, lazy, racy, mossy, posy, rosy, cosy, mercy, uneasy, daisy. Juicy, fussy, massy, intimacy, ecstasy, spicy, gypsy, tipsy. Ace, so, see, say, saw, sue, easy, owes, ooze, awes. Sighing, sewing, scion, science, sigher. Zeal, zero, czar, zinc, Zeno, Zeus.

d. Mercies, daisies, gypsies, fantasies, palsies, posies, argosies, fallacies, intimacies, piracies, policies, fancies.

e. Paucity, opposite, episode, pacify, passive, passage, bask, besought, obesity, beseech, beseige, tusk, desk. Audacity, decide, disobey, deceive, disown, dismay, russet, receive, reason, resign, Jessup, Joseph. Cusp, cossack, cask, cxcite, accede, gasp, faucet, physic, fusty, offset, effusive, vista, visit, visage, evasive, honesty, inside, unsaid, unsafe, unsung, unseen.

f. Zion, zany, zeal, zenith, zero, zinc, zodiac, zouave, czar, Zeno, Zeus.

g. Poison, basin, bison, dozen, dizen, chasten, chosen, cousin, fasten, season, Susan, lessen, arson, mason. Poisons, basins, bisons, dozens, chastens, cousins, fastens, seasons, Susan's, lessens, arsons, masons.

l. Sarah, sorrow, serious series, syrup, survey, search, serge. Sardis. service, servile, sortie, surpass, surface.

j, k. Before attempting to read lines 11 to 14, on page 17, or to write the following, learn the list of word-signs and the rules at subd. *j* and *k*. Only the new word-signs are printed in Italic below. Join the words connected by hyphens.

1. *Where-is* the-*property upon*-which they put the-*house?* 2. They *thought* he-would-come *while* we were there. 3. What-was the-*talk between* you, at the-*time* you-came *up by where* they live? 4. He *charges* too-*much*, and-it-*may-be above what* you would give. 5. I-*know no* reason why you should *hope* for it. 6. It-*is* too-*heavy* for-me. 7. *Is*-she to buy-*his house?* 8. *May* I hope I-*am* to-see you at my *house?* 9 Do you know *whether-his* book *is among* yours? 10. He-*is without*-a home, *though* he-*has* a-nice *house.*

Sec. 9. Ses.—Make the large circle about twice the size of the small one. It is seldom necessary to vocalize it.(*Lines 6, 7, p. 71*)
Mississippi, emphasis, necessary, necessity, excessive, success, exercise, exhaust, census.

a. Notice the difference between this rule and that in § 8, *d.* In the latter, the plural is formed by attaching a small circle to a stem, but in the following words, it is formed by enlarging the circle.

Pauses, poses, passes, bases, abysses, bosses, abuses, teases, tosses, adduces, cheeses, chases, chooses, cases, faces, fusses, theses, chaises, leases, laces, losses, loses, maces, misses, musses, masses, noses, noises, nooses, roses.

b. Recesses, exercises, excesses, abscesses, successes, emphasizes.

c. 1. It-is-his property. 2. I-will go as-far-as-his house. 3. Which-is-his watch, and-which-is-hers? 4. It is-as-large-as I-thought-they would-make it. 5. I-thought-so, for-his-is here. 6. Why-is-his property put there?

Sec. 10. Loops.—Make the loops carefully, and make the proper distinction between the two kinds of loops. Always place words in their proper positions. ʳRead subd. *c.* (*Line 8, page 71.*)

Steep, stoop, step, stop, stubby, state, stout, staid, stood, stitch, stage, stalk, stoke, stag. Stiff, stuff, staff, stave, steal, stale, stole, stool, star, story, stem. Pieced, paced, passed, beast, baste, boast, taste, tossed, test, dosed, dust, chased, chest, just. Feast, faced, fist, fast, vest, vast, voiced, ceased, assist, assessed, easiest, zest, leased, laced, lowest, loosed, arrest, raced, rest, rust, missed, moist, west, yeast.

Paster, pastor, poster, baster, boaster, taster, toaster, tester, duster, Chester, juster, coaster, caster, feaster, faster, foster, vaster, lustre, roster, master, muster. ʳ ʲ

b. Pests, posts, beasts, busts, tastes, tests, dusts, chests, jousts, costs, coasts, guests, gusts, feasts, fasts, vests, theists, assists, zests, arrests, rests, mists, wastes. Pasters, boasters, testers, dusters, Chester's, coasters, casters, fosters, shysters, lustres, lasters, rosters, roosters.

Piston, Posten, Liston, Justin, Masten, Weston. Pasting, boasting, toasting, dusting, jesting, casting, feasting, investing, assisting, listing, arresting, nesting, wasting, hoisting, resting.

Postern, western, southeastern. Pestering, bolstering, festering, mastering, mustering.

1. The-*company first* came *together* last *week.* 2. It-was a-*month ago.* 3. *You-are against* the-*whole party.* 4. It-was the-*common* and *usual form* of *oath.* 5. The-*first part* was put *away long-ago.* 6. I-*think* it-is *worth*-that. 7. There-is a-*large advantage* in it. 8. I-shall *recollect about* the-*thing after* you go. 9. It-is-the best we-can give. 10. What-is-their *object?* 11. *Is-there* as-much *as-there* was ?

Write the following words on the line, and omit the vowels : *Book, into, also, ask.*

Sec. 11. Subdivisions *a* and *b* contain general rules governing the use of all hooks. It is important that they be thoroughly understood.

Sec. 12. The R-Hook.—Do not make this hook any larger than it is made in the exercise on page 21. Be sure not to make it on the wrong side of the stem.

Prow, upper, bray, brow, brew, tree, tray, true, try. Troy, trow, enter, otter, outer, dray, draw, drew, dry, aider, odor, adder, odder, udder. Etcher, edger, acre, ochre, crow, crew, eager, ogre, auger, gray, grow, grew. Fray, fry, free, offer, over, ever, three, throw, through, ether, author, either, other, easer. Iser, usher, shrew, error, emir, aimer. Homer, hummer, inner.

Paper, pitcher, baker, betray, botcher, trainer. Deeper, decree, checker, chider, jabber, caper, catcher, calmer, fakir, fetcher, fiber, vigor, shader, leaper, labor, ladder. Archer, meeker, matcher, roguery, rocker, wrecker, wager.

b. Parry, opera, apiary, borrow, berry, bureau, bowery, tyro, tarry, diary, dowry, cheery, cherry, chary, carry, augury, fiery, foray, fairy, ferry, furrow, fury, sherry, showery, miry, morrow, merry, Myra, marrow, Nora, narrow, hero, Harry.

Payer, buyer, bower, dryer, briar, friar, slayer, liar, truer, cower, fewer. Prayer, tire, door, chair, fear, sheer, leer.

c. Purer, parrier, borer, bearer, barrier, burier, adorer, curer, carrier, scourer, currier, courier, firer, fairer, furrier, admirer, demurrer.

INITIAL TICKS BEFORE THE R-HOOK.

The ticks are used somewhat differently upon stems bearing hooks, than on simple stems. The outlines below are indicated by stenotypy, rules for which are given on page 56, which see. Italic capitals indicate up-strokes.

HE.—*He* cannot be prefixed by a tick to Kr, Gr, *L*r, Rr, *M*r, *H*r, or *R*r. To all other stems bearing the R-hook, *He* is prefixed by the Chay-tick.

I.—*I* is prefixed to *L*r, *M*r, and Hr, by the Ray-tick To all other stems with the R-hook, it is prefixed by the P-tick.

A,AN,AND.—Either of these words may be prefixed to Thr, Dhr, and Yr, by the T-tick. To all other stems with the R-hook, they are prefixed by the K-tick.

THE.—*The* is prefixed to Kr, Gr, *L*r, Rr, *M*r, Wr, and *H*r, by the Ray-tick ; to *N*r, *N*gr, and *R*r, by the P-tick ; to all other stems with the R-hook, by the Chay-tick.

He-appears. He-practices. He-remembers. He-tries. He-works. He-trusts. I-practice. I-remember. I-try. I-trust. I-care. I-remark. And-appear. A-number. And-remembers. A-truth. And-adjourned. A-decree. A-car. A-very. A-railroad. A-lawyer. And-work. The-proper. The-number. The-doctor. The-jury. The-decree. The-railroad. The-remark. The-manner. The-work.

1. The-*doctor's practice appears* to-be *proper.* 2. His *younger brother works* on-the *railroad.* 3. I-*remember* it-was *dark,* when the-*jury adjourned.* 4. The-*larger number* of the-*members agree.* 5. The-*lawyer* was *very-near* the-*truth* in-his *remarks.* 6. *Every* person (*P*rsn) on-the *car,* who-saw it *occur,* spoke in-that *manner.* 7. Does-he *care* to-look *over* the-*decree* any *longer?* 8. It-is *true* that the-*upper* part broke *during* the-day

d. 1. What-were-they ? 2. Which-were-said. 3. They-were by-her-side. 4 I-gave-her-money for-her-brother, who-was-with-her. 5. We-were-away. 6. He-saw-her in-her-absence. 7. Where-were-they, when-her-brother came ? 8. They-were-chosen from-her-books. 9. There-were two-or-three (Tr'Thr).

Sec. 13. The L-Hook.—Always make the L-hook small, on straight stems. On curved stems, it is made short and broad, to distinguish it from the R-hook. (*Line 9, page 71.*)

Plea, play, ply, plow, blow, blew, able, addle, idol, claw, clay, cloy, clue, eagle, glow, glue. Flee, flay, flaw, flew, evil, oval, easel, only. People, papal, puzzle. Bible, tattle, toddle, tickle, table, toggle, dapple, deploy, chapel, cheaply, cockle, cackle, camel, gavel, fickle, vocal, local, liable, label, arable, rubble, model, nickel.

c. Pillow, belic, billow, tallow, tally, daily, delay, duly, chilly, jolly, jelly, collie, coolie, gaily, gala, folly, fellow, follow, volley, valley, mellow, mallow, newly, relay, rally, holly, hollow, hilly, halo, hallow.

Baal, towel, trial, duel, dial, cruel, jewel, vial, vowel. Peel, bail, tile, jail, fall, shale, mail, kneel, reel.

d. Earl, oral, pearl, peril, parole, barrel, Farrell, thoroughly, sorrel, laurel, marl, moral, enrol, Harrell, etherial, admiral.

INITIAL TICKS BEFORE THE L-HOOK.

HE.—*He* cannot be prefixed by a tick to *L*l, Rl, Ml, Wl, or Hl. To all other stems bearing the L-hook, *He* is prefixed by the Chay-tick.

I.—*I* is prefixed to *L*l, Ml, and Hl, by the Ray-tick. To all other stems with the L-hook, it is prefixed by the P-tick.

A, AN, AND.—Either of these words may be prefixed to Chl, Jl, Thl, and Dhl, by the T-tick. To all other stems with the L-hook, they are prefixed by the K-tick.

THE.—*The* is prefixed to *L*l, Rl, Ml, Hl, and *R*l, by the Ray-tick ; to Nl and Ngl, by the P-tick ; to all other stems with the L-hook, by the Chay-tick.

He-complies. He-believed. He-tells. He-claims. He-fell. He-values. He-placed. I-apply. I-believe I-tell. I-delivered. I-rely. I-fell. I-declare. And-compel. And-belonged. A-belief. An-angel. An-equal. A-delivery. And-fill. And-really. A-rule. A-wealthy. And-disclaimed. The-people. The-delivery. The-claim. The-value. The-rule. The-wealth.

1. I-*believe* he-will *really compel* the-*people* to *comply fully* with the-*rule.* 2. The-*clerk claimed* to have *delivered* the-*roll* to the-*children.* 3. He *relies* upon-his *claim* that he-*fell* on-the *rail.* 4. *Tell* him to *call,* and I-will *deliver* property *equal* to-that in *value.* 5. He *declares*-his *belief* that their *wealth* was *real,* but-that it *belonged largely* to their *children.* 6. They will make the-*delivery* by *degrees.* 7. *Fill* it *full.*

e. 1. It-will-be as-well, after-all, to *apply* soon. 2. Which-will you take, of-all they offer ? 3. They-will-go, if you-will. 4. What-will-they do with-all-those boxes ? 5. She-will do the-work as-well-.as he does-it.

Sec. 14. When circles are combined with hooks, the combinations are named Sper, Spel, Sfer, Sfel, etc. When the small loop is thus combined, the outlines are called Stepr, Stetr, etc. The loops cannot be combined with hooks on curved stems, and Ses is never combined with a hook at the beginning of an outline. In writing circles within hooks on curved stems, care should be taken not to change the size of the hook. (*Lines 10-12, page 71.*)

Spray, spry, sapper, supper, sober, saber, stray, straw, strew, suitor, sitter, setter, cedar, sadder, cider, sager, sicker, soaker, safer, cypher, suffer, savor, scaler, simmer, saner, signer, singer. Stopper, stupor, stabber, stater, staider, stitcher, .stager, sticker, stoker, stalker, stagger.

a. Supple, supply, sable, settle, saddle, sidle, satchel, sickle, cycle, civil, sizzle, social.

d. It occasionally happens that a hook cannot be made exact, when preceded by a circle in the middle of an outline. Care should be taken, in such cases, that it be sufficiently indicated.

Pastry, besieger, tasker, decipher, destroy, descry, disagree, gossamer, vestry, vesper, massacre, mastery, extra. Peaceable, paschal, disclose, disciple, disable, explosive, gospel, physical, visible, useful.

Sec. 15. Do not pass this section without understanding it perfectly. It provides the only means of indicating vowels between stems and their initial hooks. Do not leave it so carelessly as to make it possible for you to attempt to apply the rule to final hooks hereafter. *It does not apply to final hooks.*

Partial, paraphrase, parsimony, perceive, purple, dark, cheerful, Charles, journey, journal, church, kernel, courage, course, excursive, nearly, more, tell. till, delicacy, call, cull, cool, college, calumny, unskilful, fill, fell, fulfil, falsify, volume, valuable, vulgar, village, vulnerable.

How may be indicated, at the beginning of a phrase, by either the Chay- or Ray-tick, but the tick is always written immediately below the line.

How-much. How-long. How-many. How-far How-wide. How-can. How-true.

1. The-*judge committed* the-defendant. 2. *Ah*, Mary, you *forget* that-we *already once* the-*agent's wife* a-*dollar*. 3. He *gave*-us his *age*. 4. The-*youth* who *accompanied* him was *worthy* of notice. 5. They *occupy* the farm which *adjoins* his, *but* they-are in *different counties*.

Sec. 16. The N-Hook.—Make the hook small, on both straight and curved stems. This hook cannot be used, when the sound of N is followed by a vowel at the end of a word. (*Lines 13, 14, p. 71.*)

Pine, spine, pun, plain, prone. Spain, pan, plan, bin, brain, blown, tone, train, stain. Dane, done, sudden, drown, chain, join. June, keen, crane, clown, skin, screen, gain, grown, fawn. Often, stiffen, vain, even, seven. Thane, thin, then, assign, sheen, shine, sullen, slain, lawn, earn, stern (stRn), reign. Rhine, mean, moan, Simon, marine, moon, known, noon, swain, swan, one. wine, yawn. Pekin, pippin, pigeon, pennon (PnN), bacon, beaten. Buffon, obtain, bemoan, balloon, tighten, ottoman, detain, dungeon, domain. Chicken. cheapen, kitchen, cunning, griffin, gammon, foeman, vanish (Vn*Sh*), linen.

b. Olean, alien, ruin, galleon, scion. Pretorian, grammarian, agrarian, valerian, censorian, clarion.

c. Pines, spines, sprains, bones, bans, buns, tones, trains, stains, strains (sTrns), dins, dense, drowns, Siddons, chains, chance, joins, canes, coins, gains, groans, glance. Johnson, Robinson, Wisconsin, Benson's.

d. Pounced, pranced, bounced, danced, chanced, glanced. Spinster, punster, spinsters, punsters.

e. Princes, prances, pounces, bounces, trounces, dunces, chances, sconces, cleanses, glances.

f. Fence, softens, fawns, veins, heavens, Athens, thence, assigns, oceans, shuns, shines, lens, loans, lance, rains, rinse, runs, moans, immense, nonce, announce, wines.

FINAL TICKS AFTER THE N-HOOK.

HE, THE.—Use the Ray-tick for *He* or *The*, after Fn, Vn, Sn, and Ngn ; the P-tick after Kn, Gn, Thn, Dhn, *L*n, Mn, Yn, Hn, and *R*n. Use the Chay-tick for either of these words, after any other N-hook combination.

I.—Use the T-tick only, for *I*.

A, AN, AND.—Use the K- or T-tick, choosing that one which will make the best angle with the hook.

Even-he. Again-he. Then-he. Combine-the. Taken-the. Imagine-the. Connect-the. Forgotten-the. Within-the. Lengthen-the. Within-a. Then-an.

1. The-*man* has-been *connected* with the-*bank continuously*, since-it-was *organized*. 2. If-they *combine* and-*organize*, I-*imagine* the-trouble will *continue* as it has *begun*. 3. *Within*-a week, the stock has-been *generally taken*, by-*men* of *financial* ability, and-they will

begin at-once to *organize* the-company, with-a new *constitution.*
4. His-disease is *organic*, and-his-pain has-been *continuous* since-it
began. 5. The-*divine* law is the-basis of what-has-been *denominated
human* law. 6. To some, the-duties of *religion* are a-*continual
punishment.*

g. Before-and-after. For-an-hour. Did-not-have. Come-and-
go. Cannot-be. Give-an-opinion. Your-own. Our-own. More-
than. Up-and-down. Thought-not. May-not-have. Did-not-be.
Cannot-I. Was-not-that.

Sec. 17. The F-Hook.—This hook is made small, on straight
stems, and on the L-hook side of the stem. On curved stems, it is
made long and narrow, to distinguish it from the N-hook. It will
require care to make it accurately, but after a little practice it may
be made readily and correctly. It should be made as if it were to be
a large loop, but without closing the loop. (*Lines 15, 16, page 71.*)

Pave, approve, puff, beef, brief, bluff, tough, dove, drove, chief,
chafe, chaff. Jove cuff, cliff, crave, carve, grief, grove, leaf,
slave, lave, luff, laugh. Reef, rave, roof, move, niff, muff, knave.
Knife, enough, weave, woof, spavin. Tiffany, divine, achieving,
jovial, cover, govern, lover, river, revery, nymph, traffic.

a. Paves, puffs, beeves, doves, defense, coves, raves, moves,
knives, slaves.

FINAL TICKS AFTER THE F-HOOK.

HE, THE.—Use the Chay-tick for *He* or *The*, after Sf, Zf, Shf,
Zhf, Rf, and Wf ; the Ray-tick after Pf, Bf, Kf, Gf, Ff, Vf, Nf,
Ngf, and Rf. Use the P-tick for either of these words after any
other F-hook combination.

I.—Use the T-tick only, for *I.*

A,AN,AND.—Use the K- or T-tick, choosing that one which
will make the best angle with the hook.

Whatever-he. Hope-to-have-the. Whatever-I. Perform-an.
Refer-a. Thoughtful-and.

1. *Whatever* success you *hope-to-have* from the-*performance,*
I-*advise* you to *refer* to him for-his *opinion*, and to be *governed* by-his
advice. 2. His-*deformity* is *objective.* but the-pain he-suffers is
subjective and-*difficult* to prove. 3 His early *poverty developed* a-
thoughtful care. 4 His *language developes nothing new* upon the-
issue. 5. *They-are young*, but *you-are now* well *along* in *years.* and
cannot *perform* such labor. 6. *To-whom* do you *refer?* 7. He-is
beyond recovery, I-am *advised.*

c. Part-of. What-have-been. It-will-have. Difference-of-opinion. Ever-have. Have-ever. They-have-known. So-have. I-shall-have. He-should-have. May-have. Know-of. Think-of. We-have.

d. Fifing, thieving, shoving, leaving, moving, weaving. Ever-have-been. Have-ever-been. They-have-been. I-shall-have-been. He-will-have-been. It-may-have-been. We-have-been. You-have-been.

Sec. 18. The Y-Hook.—As stated in the rule, this hook is used only for phrasing purposes. On straight stems, it is made twice the size of the R-hook. On a curved stem, it is made of the exact shape of the F-hook on curves, but it is only used initially.

Upon-your-own. Pay-your-money. Before-you-know. Do-you-not-know? Had-you-ever-been? Did-you-state? Which-you-have. Can-you-state? If-you-do. Have-you-not-been? Should-you-say-so? May-you-not-be? In-your-opinion. Would-you-not-say? What-year.

a. What-will-you? Where-will-you-go? Either-you or-your brother. In-that-year. Or-will-you. Where-were-you?

Sec. 19. The W-Hook.—This hook is made twice the size of the L-hook. It is not used on curved stems.

Twins, twain, twice, twenty, twig, Edwin, dwell, quaff, queen, quince, squeak, squib, squash, quiver, quill, queer, Gwinn, quarrel, squirrel, query, quest, quail, square.

a. Upon-what-is-that? Before-we-may-have. But-whether-they-have. What-we-have-been. What-would-you? But-what-is-that? Do-we-not-know? Had-we-ever-been. Can-we-not-go? Or-whether-it-was. Are-we-not?

b. Would-be. We-would. That-we-were. Nor-were-we. If-you-were. I-wish-you-would-go.

1. He-was *quartered* in-that *dwelling*. 2. They *acquiesced*, as-soon-as-the *question* arose. 3. He-*dwelt* near-the *railway*. 4. Do-not *dwell* too long on-the *question*, if-they *acquiesce*. 5. The-noise *bewilders* her.

Sec. 20. The Ter-Hook.—This hook is made on the N-hook side of any straight stem, and is twice the size of that hook. It adds to the stem the syllable Ter, Der, or Ther.

Peter, platter, potter, splutter, beater, bather, bitter, bother, blotter, braider, tighter, traitor, tatters, chatter, crater, clatter, gaiter.

a, b. Patters, praters, bothers, braiders, blotters, daughters, debtors, caters, glitters. Battering, pottering, tottering, chattering, glittering, clattering, guttering.

c. Upon-all-their. About-what-they-are. At-all-their. Do-their-best. Change-their. Can-there-be? Go-there.

Sec. 21. The M-Hook.—This is also a large hook, and is' made on the F-hook side of any straight stem, or on the inside of a curved stem. Make it short and broad.

Palm, prim, prime, plum, balm, bomb, broom, bloom. Brim, team. tame, tomb, trim, tramway. Dim, dumb, dream, dram, chum, chime. Jim, gems, jam, calm, comb, cam, crime, clime, crumb, chrome. Gleam, groom, grim, gloom, fame, foam, vim. Thumb, them, sachem, shame, sham, limb, lame, loam. Slam, lime, arm, rim, room, roam, rhymes. Maim, ma'am, mum, mummery, name, gnome.

a. Primes, brooms, blooms, teams, trims, dreams, chimes, gems, crimes, clams, foams, shames, slams, maims, names. Priming, teaming, chiming, charming, foaming, shamming, naming.

b. Premium, delirium, encomium, equilibrium, emporium.

c. Upon-him. It-may-be. What-time. Watch-him. For-him. With-him. At-that-time. Did-you-make-known. For-my-sake.

d. By-their-own. Better-than. Rather-than. Upon-my-own. Ever-have-been. We-have-been. For-my-own. At-their-own.

1. He-was *commissioned* soon after-he-was *nominated.* 2. The-*commissioner* did-not *discriminate* between the-*memoranda* which-were produced. 3. I-was *familiar* with the-*family*, for-*some-time.* 4. They-will *themselves* make-a *memorandum* of the-*minimum* price. 5. They cannot-be forced to *criminate themselves.*

Sec. 22. The Tion-Hook.—Make the circle small, and draw the back-hook close to the stem.

Potion, passion, option, edition, addition, auction, caution, occasion, action. Fashion. fusion, evasion, vision, ovation, session, elision, elation, illusion, allusion. Oration, erosion, ration, mission, emotion, nation, notion, unction. Petition. palliation, pollution, ablution, ebullition, tertian, education, adoption, devotion, admission. Delusion, adulation, adoration, ejection, junction. Fiction, affection, faction, affliction, function. Vacation, avocation, variation, location, legation, elevation, erection. Irrigation, rotation, imitation, magician, monition, ammunition, notation, invasion.

Potions, editions, cautions, actions, fashions, visions, sessions, allusions, portions (PRsns), narrations.

Expansion, detention, declension, pension, abstention, suspension, tension, extension, distension.

b. Professional, optional, exceptional, educational. Devotional, sectional, factional, functional, emotional, national, notional. Petitioner, stationary, dictionary, auctioneer, electioneer, visionary.

c. Petitioned, pensioned, proportioned, cautioned, occasioned, motioned, fashioned. Proportionate, affectionate, passionate.

d. Causation, accession, accusation, precision, procession, physician, cessation, incision, musician. Accessions, decisions, processions. Processional, sensational.

e, f. Transition, concession (Knssn), dispensation, condensation (*with Con-dot*), compensation, organization. Transitional. Fusionist, visionist, factionist, elocutionist.

1. Before the *decision*, there-was much *opposition* to-his *occupation* of the-*position* in the-*organization* for-which-he had-been given the-*nomination*. 2. It-is-my-*recollection* that the-*adoption* of the-*resolution* by the-*institution* was *conditional* upon the-*continuation* of-his *connection* with the-*denomination*. 3. *Additional information* comes to our *attention*, which fixes the-*conviction* that the-*contention* of-that portion of the-*denomination* will-be-sure to take from him the
· *possession* of that *position*.

Sec. 23. Halving.—The student will recognize the importance of making his stems accurate in length, that he may have no difficulty in distinguishing half-lengths. It is also necessary that care be taken to make the different hooks and circles of proper size, on half-lengths. The first position for half-lengths, is at the height of a T-stem above the line ; and the third position is immediately below but touching the line of writing. (*Line 17, page 71.*)

Peat, pet, pat, bead, bid, bud, bowed, taught. Tight, deed, date, dude, cheat, chat, jawed, caught, coat. Cute, gait, goad, get, God, good, fate, fought, fat, foot. Evade, vat, vied, vowed, viewed, east, oust, eased, oozed. Sheet, shoot, shot, shut, load, laid, let, lot, light, allowed, art, heart, erred. / Rate, wrought, wrote, write, rut. Meet, made, might, need, note, weed, wait, wooed, yacht.

Pride, plate, pained, puffed, pattered, palmed, supped. Braid, blood, bend, abaft, sobbed. Treat, told, tuned, tuft, sighted. Dried, addled, dunned, daft, dimmed, sodded. Cheered, chained, chilled, achieved, chimed, chattered, charred. Joined, jammed. Cried, cold, conned, coughed, catered, calmed, skate, scanned. Agreed, glad, gained, gift, gathered, gummed. Fright, flat, faint, fifed, fumed, soft, feats. Averred, valued, vend, saved, vats; vents. Thread, thinned, theft, thumbed, soothed. Shield, shunned, shift, shamed, shoots. Lord, lined, left, loomed, lights, slight. Errand, armed, arts, seared. Rolled, round, rift, roomed, rights. Mind, muffed, maimed, meets. Neared, knifed, named, needs. Word, wield, wind, waved, swayed. Yield.

a. Sent. Send. Let. Laid. Lent. Lend. Met. Made. Meant. Mend. Hurt. Heard.

d. When it is desired to distinguish the sounds of T and D, in halving Ray (as in the words *fort* and *ford*), the stem may be slightly shaded for the latter sound.

Pillared, feared, veered, leered, laird, lard, lured, fort, ford, afford, lowered, mired. Kindred (Knd*R*d¹), covered (Kv*R*d).

e. Motive, talkative, active, ablative, operative, susceptive, adjective, elective, captive, negative, provocative, speculative, lucrative, figurative, defective, productive, native, destructive, irruptive.

f. Upon-the-occasion. Pay-the-money. By-the-time. Before-it-came. At-the-same-time. To-the-master. Did-it-mean. Had-the-time. Can-it-be. For-it-was-not. Of-the-service. Any-of-the-time. Some-of-it. Part-of-the-time (Pft³M). Give-to-him.

g. What-did-he. He-did-not (Hd¹Nt). She-did-not. You-did. That-did. We-did. They-did. When-did-you-go ? Why-did-you-leave ? Where-did-he-live ? How-did-you ? In-what-way. For-what-purpose (FtPr). From-what-time.

1. *According-to*-his statement, they-had a-*particular opportunity* to *understand* what-the *gentleman* meant, but *notwithstanding*-that, it-seemed that *nobody* in-the *neighborhood quite understood* it.   2. You-will-not *need* it *immediately*.   3. I-shall-be-*able-to build* the-*building toward* fall.   4. A-*good*-man might-be *somewhat negligent*, but he-*could-not*-be *guilty* of-such *neglect* as-that.   5. *Anybody* would *accept* such-an *opportunity*, I-am-*pretty*-sure, *except* an-*individual mentally* deficient (DfSh), by *nature*, as he-seems to be.   6. The-*expenditure* was-not *under* a-*hundred*-dollars.

Sec. 24. Lengthening—Father, finder, flounder, vendor, thither, aster, asunder, shatter, shouter, slighter, slender, laughter, ardor, mother, smatter, mentor, another, wonder, hunter, reënter, inventor, dissenter, defender.

Frequenter, enchanter, taunter, encounter, plunders, blinders, glanders.

b. Been-there. Done-there. Cannot-there. Gone-there. For-there-has-been (Ftrsn). Have-there-been. Of-their. Thought-there. With-their. See-there. May-there. In-there. Without-their. When-they-are. The-other (Dhtr). Some-other (sMtr).

Sec. 25. a.—Rented, gifted, wounded, dated, goaded, intended, cheated, invited, rotated, coated, estimated, separated. Potted, braided, budded, shouted, spotted, mended, vaunted, shunted. Ascended, hated, landed, counted, banded, weeded, tufted. Lighted, plotted, omitted, blighted, surrounded, invaded, rewarded.

Posted, boasted, breasted, toasted, twisted, digested, detested, jested, coasted, crested. Manifested, feasted, invested, harvested, listed, ballasted, arrested, wasted.

Pestered, plastered, blistered, blustered, registered. Festered, bolstered, mastered, mustered.

b. Read the rule carefully, and read "The Choice of Outlines," page 70. See, also, illustrative words on page 64.

h. Destruction, distraction, obstruction, abstraction, application, attainment, assignment, contract, attract, contraction, attraction, achievement, fact, effect, afflict, affliction, darkness, electricity, obligation.

Consonants may often be omitted in other classes of words than those heretofore mentioned, but the writer should be governed by the rule that nothing should be omitted which is essential to the perfect legibility of the outline. It is generally safe to omit a consonant which is sounded but slightly, if a better outline may be secured by so doing. The following examples will suggest the proper application of this expedient :

Mostly, MsL. Postal, PsL. Specification, sPsFsn. Ratification, Rt^3Fsn. Attempt, TMt. Dumped, DMt. Anxious, NgShs^3. Sanction, sNgsn^3. Assumption, S^{3}Msn. Improvement, MPr^{3}Mnt. Slightest, sLtst^1. Brightest, Brtst^1. Chamber, ChBr. Timber, TBr. Lumber, LmR. Slumber, sLmR. Intelligence, NtJns. Arrangement, RMnt. Typewriter, TRtr. Inspect, NsPt. Reject, RJt. Forgiven, FGn.

l. Where the stem Ng can be used as conveniently, the backhook should not be used for the termination -*ing.*

Premising, epitomising, prancing, debasing, dispensing, dancing, chastising, temporizing, transposing, endorsing (NdRsn), surmising, using.

Proceeding, prickling, prevailing, sprinkling, breathing, dumpling, shearing, shelving.

m. Came-to-Syracuse. Difficult-to-understand. Brought-it-to-me. About-to-be. Soon-to-begin. Sure-to-be-able-to. Hope-to-be-there. Give-that-to-them. Trouble-to-change.

Strange to-say. Willing to-state. Read-it to-him. Show-it to-her. Good-news to-all-men. Given to-you. Went to-the-market. Gone to-their-house.

I. It-is-to-be hoped that *intelligent* and-*independent* electors will-not forget-the-*fact* that-such-men are *behind* the-*movement.* 2. Within a-*day-or-two*, we-shall-have a-*contract* for-a large *quantity*, which-we hope will-have the-*effect* of *attracting trade.* 3. They-had no *authority*-to-*direct* that-it-should-be *examined.* 4. He *remarked, with-regard-to*-the new supply of *water*, that-it would-be-a *year-or-two* before-it-could-be obtained. 5.. It-is *frequently mentioned* among-his *acquaintances, yet* he-continues-to-act *without-regard-to*-the *importance* of-the-subject. 6. It was *decreed* that the *convict* should be *subjected* to a punishment *measured* by the grade of his crime.

Sec. 26. Prefixes and Affixes.—Accommodate. Competition, contrition, concussion. Unconfined, incumbency, recognize. Controvert, countermand, contradict. Foreborne, forward. Instrument, unsalable. Introduction, introvert, enterprise. Magnetism. Relator. Selfabased; selfdenial. Thereby, therefor, thereafter. Unable, invincible. Seasonableness. Docketed, tidied, dictated. Essential, penitential. Whichever. whosoever, whensoever. Therefore, uniform. Thankful, wrongful. Disdainful, graceful, brimful, sinful. Impressing, pottering, dreaming, removing. Drawing. Provokingly, exceedingly. Trying-a, growing-an. Drawing-the, raking-the. Beings, doings. Probability, popularity. Visibility, legality, minority, rascality, neutrality. Boundlessness, worthlessness. Sacramental. Doxology. Typographer, bibliography. Himself, itself, for-itself, themselves. Lordship. Cleanly, sorely.

Disjoined stems must be written *very near* the remainder of the outline.

Sec. 27. i. In-this-statement, NThssTtMnt. For-example, FsMPl. I-may-as-well, *p*MsL. In-writing, Nrt¹Ng. Hand-writing, Nrt³Ng. At-any-rate, TNrt. At-all-events, TlvNts. At-length, Tln. Most-likely, MsLKl. Most-of-the-time, MsM. It-must-be, TMsB. Some-of-the-time, sMM. According-to-my-recollection, Krd¹M*R*sn. Some-other, sMtr. In-the-conversation, NtVssn. Are-engaged, *R*n³G. I-call-your-attention, *p*KlYsn. Called-my-attention, Kld¹Msn. In-that-season, NThssn³. In-his-house, Nss¹. I-don't-know-as-I-do, *r*DnNsD. What-is-the-matter, Ts¹Mtr. Lake-street, .LKst. In-my-store, N¹Mstr.

q. · Upon-him. With-him. Offend-him. Lend-him. Attend-him. Pain-him.

r. By-himself. To-himself. For-himself. With-himself. Against-himself. ·

s. At-one. But-one. Each-one. Which-one. Any-one. No-one. Long-one. Every-one. Either-one. Other-one. Only-one.

t. The-base-is. The-case-is. Buys-his. Knows-his. It-is-as-large. ·

u. In-the-spring. In-the-summer. In-the-same-place. In-consideration of-that.

v. It-should-be. I-should-think. He-should-not-have. We-should-not.

w. I-have (*tv*¹). I-say. He-is. He-has. On-his. All-is. All-has-been. Who-were. Who-will. Who-have. Who-is (*or* has).

x. Piece-of-land. What-time-of-day. State-of-Maine. Justice-of-the-peace (JsPs).

y. 20 or 30. 17 or 18 hundred-dollars. From 7 to 10. Between 5 and 6 thousand.

WORDS ENDING WITH L.

The figures give the positions of the outlines. The signs indicated by small capitals should be inserted.

HOOK L.	DOWNWARD L.	UPWARD L.
1. Comply, ply, plea.	Pall, ap-peal, pile, pill.	Pillow.
2. People, compel, play.	Pale, pail, pole, poll.	Haply.
3. Apply, apple, plow.	Pull, pool. -	Happily, pulley.
1. Belong-ed, by all.	Ball, bill, boil, bile.	Belie, bailee, by-law.
2. Belief-ve-d, able-y.	Bale, bail, bell, bowl.	Below, bellow, belay.
3. Blue, blew, about all.	Bull, buhl.	Bully.
1. Tall, what will.	TEal, tile, toil.	
2. Till, tell, it will, at all.	Tale, tail, toll.	At law.
3. Tool, to all, but will.	Towel.	Tallow, tally, outlaw.
1. Idol, idle, idyll, did all.	Deal, doll, dial, Ideal.	Differently, Ideally, oddly.
2. Deliver-ed-y, do all.	Dale, dole, conDole, dell,	Daily, dahlia, delay.
3. Addle, had all.	Dual, duel, dowel. [dull.	Dally, duly.
1. Each will, watch all.	Chill.	Chilly.
2. Children, which will.		
3. Much will, charge all.		
1.	Congeal, gill.	Jolly.
2. Angel.	Jail.	Jelly.
3. Largely, agile.	Jewel, jowl.	July.
1. Equal-ed, call, kill, cloY	Commonly, keel, chyle,	Common law, collie,
2. Claim-ed, coal, clay-ey.	Kail. caul, coil.	[key-Hole.
3. Clerk, cool, clue.		Coolie, callow.
1. Eagle, glee.	Gall, gill, gurle.	
2. Ugly, ogle.	Gale, goal, gull.	Gala, gaily, gully.
3. Glue.	Ghoul.	Galley.
1. Fill, flEE, flaw, awful-ly	Feel, fall, file, foil.	Filly, folly.
2. Fell, flAY, flow.	Fail, foul.	Folio, fellow, follow.
3. Full-y, flue, flew.	Fool, fuel, fowl.	Fallow.
1. Evil, of all.	Veal, vile, viol, vial.	Villa, volley.
2. Oval.	Avail, veil, vale.	Heavily.
3. Value.	Vowel, avowal.	Valley, uvula.
1. Little.		LEal, loyal, lily, loll.
2. Lull.		Lowly, ill-will.
1. *Rely, real-ly, or all.	*Reel, rIll, royal.	*Royally.
2. *Rail, oral-ly, there will.		*Relay.
3. *Rule, are all.	*Rowel.	*Rally.
1. †From all.		‡Aerial, aurelia.
2. †Earl.		‡Early, airily, airHole.
3.		‡Hourly. [oriel.
1.	Timely.	Meal-y, mall, mill, mile.
2. May all.		Mail, melee, mellow,
3. Mal.		Mallow, mule. [mole.
1. In all.	Kneel, Anneal, nil.	Nolle.
2. Only, null, know all.	Nail, knell, knoll, Annul.	Inlay, nulla.
3. Knew all.	Annual-ly.	Newly.
1. Wall, awhile.	lWeal.	Wile-y, willow.
2.	lWail, well (of water.)	Waylay.
3. Wool-ly.		Wallow.
1.	¶Heal, haul, hall, hill-y.	Holly.
2. When will.	¶Hail, hale, hell, hull.	Hollow, holloa, halo.
3. How will.	¶Howl.	Hallow, halloo.

* Written with Ray.   † Written with Ar.   ‡ Ar-Lay.   l Written with semi-circle.   ¶ Written with H-tick and Lay.

WORDS ENDING WITH R.

The figures give the positions of the outlines. The signs indicated by small capitals should be inserted.

HOOK R.	DOWNWARD R.	UPWARD R.
1. Appear, proper, pry.	Com-peer, pier, pyre.	Opera, parLAH, peri.
2. Upper, pray, prey,pro.	Com-pare, pour, payer.	Apiary.
3. Practice, prow.	Happier, poor, power.	Pure, parry.
1. Liberty.	Beer, bier, buyer. [er.	Borrow.
2. Remember.	Bear, bore, burr, obEY-	Bury, burrow, borough.
3. Brother, number, brEw.	Bar, boor, bower.	Barrow, bureau, bowery
1. Internal, tree, Eater.	Tier, tear, at-tire.	Tyro, tiara.
2. Truth, tray, utter.	Tare, tear, tore.	Terra, tory.
3. True, outer, coNtra.	Tar, coN-tour, tower.	Tarry.
1. Dear, dry, draw, Eider.	Deer, commodore, dire.	Diarrhœa, diary.
2. Doctor, dray, odor.	Dare, doer, door, adore.	Dairy, dory.
3. During, dark, drew.	Dower.	Dowry.
1. Watcher, cheer.		Cheery.
2. Etcher, chair.	Chore.	Chary, cherry.
3. Char.		
1. Conjure.	Jeer, objector.	
2. Adjourn-ed.	Ajar.	
3. Jury, larger, junior.	Jar, adjure.	
1. Decree, erAw, cry.		
2. Care, occur, concur.	Core, corps, cohEir.	Curry.
3. Car,cure,crew,accrue.	Cower.	Carry.
1. Agree, degree, augur.	Gear, giver.	Augury.
2. Gray, grow, ogre.	Gore, goer.	Gory.
3. Grew.		
1. Offer, free, fry.	Fear, A-fire.	Fiery. [furrow, furry.
2. Fray, fro, confer.	Af-fair, A-fore, fur, fir.	Fairy, faro, foray, ferry,
3. Affray.	Fewer, A-far.	Farrow, fury.
1. Over, of her.	Veer.	Ivory.
2. Every, very, Hover.	Conveyor.	Vary, Aviary, ovary.
3. Aver.	Viewer, avower.	Avowry.
1. Wisher.	Sheer, shear, shire.	
2. Usher.	Share, A-shore, shower.	Sherry.
3. Sure, shrew.	Shower, assure.	Showery, ashery.
1. Lawyer.	Liar, lier, lyre, leer.	
2.	Lair, layer, lower, lore.	*Allayer.
3.	Lure, lower (to threaten)	*Allure.
1. +Or were.		‡Orrery.
2. +Railroad, there were.		‡Aurora.
1. ‖From her.	¶Arrear, from our.	**Rear.
2. ‖Error, where were.	¶Where our.	**Roar, rower, rare.
1. Mere.	Mire.	Miry, morrow.
2. More,aimer, Hummer.	Mayor, mare, myrrh. .	Mower, Emery, merry.
3. Mar, humor..	Moor, amour.	Marry, marrow.
1. Near, nor, honor, in-	Nigher, annoYer.	
2. Manner. [ner.	Ne'er.	Narrow.
3. Owner.	Newer, inure.	
1. We were.	Wire, weir.	Wiry, we are.
2. Work.	Wore, wear, a-ware.	Worry, wary.
3.	Wooer.	
2.	War (with semi-circle.)	
1.	++Hire, higher.	++Hero,
2. When were.	++Hair-Y, hoar.	++Hoary, hurry.
3. How were.	++Hewer.	++Harrow.

* El-Ar.   + Written with Ray.   ‡ Ar-Ray.   ‖ Written with Ar.
¶ Ar-Ar.   ** Ray-Ray.   ++ H-tick.

ILLUSTRATIVE PHRASES.

All the other, bDhtr
All we were doing, bwwDng
Although it is not much more than [bDhtaNtChMn
Although we were, bDhww
Always has been, Wssn¹
Am not to be, Mn³B
And his wife, ksF¹
And so forth, ks³F
And is the, ksch¹
Another way, Ntrw
Any other way, NjW
Any part of it, NP¹ft¹
Anything further, NNgFtr
Are you aware, Ry³Wr
Are you certain about it, RysRtBt
As a matter of fact, sMtr²Ft
As far as possible, sFs³Ps
As far as they have been, sFs³Dhvn
As it has been, Ztsn³
As it seems to me, Zts³MsM
As soon as you have been, ssNs³Yvn
As to what would be, Zt³uwB
As we have been, s³Wvn
As you have stated, s³Yvst
Ask his attention, SKsTsn
At my office, TmFs
At or about the time, TrBtM
At some time or other, TsMmRtr
At the present time, TtPrsM
Attract (ed) my attention, Trt³Msn
Because we have, Ks¹wV
Best of my recollection, BsMRsn
Best recollection, BstRsn
Board of trade, BrdTrd
Branch of the case, BrNChtKs
Brother in law, Br³Nl
Burden of proof, BrdPrf
But as has been, Tssn³
But you may have been, Ty³Mvn
By the way, Bt¹W, or Btw¹
By virtue of, B¹Vr
Call forth, Klf¹
Call my attention, KlMsn⁴
Call their attention, Kltrsn¹
Call your attention, KlYsn³
Come (Came) away, Kw
Came there, Ktr
Can we not, Kwn³
Can you state, Kyst³
Cannot recollect, KnR¹
Cannot remember, Kn³B
Cannot say, Kns³
Cannot state, Knst³
Cause and effect, KsFt¹
Certain circumstances, sRtsTnss
Clerk's office, Kls³Fs [KltR¹³sTnss
Collateral circumstances,

Common carrier, KKRr¹
Common council, KKsL¹
Could not (Couldn't) say, KdNts
Could not tell you, KdNtLy
Course of business, Krs³Bss
Cross examination, Krssn¹
Did he ever have, Dr¹Vv
Did you ever know, Dyv¹N
Did you have any conversation, [Dyv¹NVssn
Did you not say, Dyns¹
Did you not state, Dynst¹
Did we not say, Dwns¹
Difference of opinion, Df¹Nn
Direct examination, DrtsMsn
Do you know him, Dy¹Nm
Does he ever, DsrV
Down stairs, Dnstrs³
During the time, Drt³M
Each of them, Chv¹Dhm
Easier than, Z¹Rn
Enclose their, NKlstr
End of it (the), Nd³Vt
Entitled to a verdict, NTVrd
Et cetera, TsTR
Everywhere else, VrRLs
Faster than, Fstrn³
For an instant, FnNsTnt
For interest, Fnt
For several years, FsVy
For some time, FsMm
For the purpose (of) FtPr
Friday morning, FrDM
From hour to hour, R³-R
From time to time, MM¹
Future state, F¹Chrst
Gave it to them, Gt³Dhm
Glad of it, Gld³Vt
Good deal of, Gd²Lv
Greater or less, Grt²Ls
Had been there, D³Btr
Had their attention, Dtrsn³
Has been done, s³BnDn
Has been stated, s³Bnst
Has not been there, sNt³Btr
Have had the opportunity, Vd³chPrt
Have you stated, Vyst³
He had, Hd³
He did it, Hdr¹
He did not say that, HdNtsDh³
He did not state, HdNtst¹
He has been, cha²Bn
He has been there, chs²Btr
He may have been, chMvn
He must have been, chMstn
He said to me, chsDtM
He was not there, chZntr
Her testimony, RtsMN
Hope to find it, PtFndr

How are we, *chRw*³
How did he, Hdr³
How did you ever, Hd*y*³V
How have you, *ch*³Vy
How is it, Hst³
How long after that, *r*Ng³FDh
How long before, *r*Ng³B
How long have you been, *r*Ng³Bn
How long have you resided there, *r*Ngst³   [*r*Ng³sDtr
How long is it, *r*Ngst³
How many times, *ch*³MNms
How much money, *r*³ChMN
Human life, Mn³F
I am certain, *p*M⁴sRt
I am not in the habit of, *p*Mn³NtBt
I am not positive, *p*Mn³Pst
I am pretty sure, *p*M³PrtShr
I am sure there is, *p*M³Shrtrs
I believe he did not state, *p*BlHdNtst
I believe he was not there, *p*Bl*ch*Zntr
I believe they did say that, [*p*BlDhdsDh
I call your attention, *p*KlYsn
I called his attention, *p*KldsTsn
I cannot remember the time, [*r*Kn³BtM
I could not say positively, *r*KdNtsPst
I could not tell you, *r*Kd³NtL*y*
I do not remember the conversation, I have stated, *r*Vst³   [*r*DnBtVrssn
I heard him say so, t*R*dHsS
I know about the time, *r*N³BtM
I mean to be, *p*MnB
I meant to say, *p*Mnt³S
I need not tell you, *r*Nd¹NtL*y*
I never did say that, *r*NvdsDh
I shall have been, *r*Shvn
I should say it was, *r*Sh³StZ
I suppose you did, *r*sPsYd
I take the opportunity, *r*TtPrt
I think there were, *r*Ngtrw¹
I think they did, *r*Ng¹Dhd
I want to know, tWnt¹N
I wish to know, *r*Sht¹N
I was not there, *r*Zntr
If he should say, F¹*ch*Shs
If it is possible, Fts¹Ps
If it were, Ft*w*¹
If she did not, F¹ShdNt
If there were, Ftr*w*¹
In all circumstances, Nl¹sTnss
In all respects, NlsPs
In all such cases, Nl¹sChKss
In all they did, Nl¹Dhd
In continuation (of), NKnsn¹
In his judgment, NsJ³Mnt
In other words, NjWds¹
In point of fact, N¹PntFt
In the afternoon, NtF³Nn
In the forenoon, NtF³Nn
In the month of, NtThv

In the daytime, NtDm
In the night time, NtNtTm
In the world, Nt¹Rld
In their possession, NtrPssn
In what position, NtPssn
In your opinion, NyNn¹
Is it possible, Zt¹Ps
Is there anybody, strNBd¹*
Is there not, strNt¹*
Is to be, Zt¹B
It has been stated, TsBnst
It is just as possible, TsJstsPs
It may as well, TMsL
It may not have been, TMnBn
It must have been, TMstn
It will not be, TlnB
It will have to be, TlvB
Just about the time, JsBtM
Just after they did it, JstFDhd*ch*
Just so, JsS
Just such, JssCh
Knows nothing about it, NsNgBt
Knows that we were, Ns³Dh*ww*
Knows we were, Ns³*ww*
Ladies and gentlemen, LDsJnt
Larger than, Jrn³
Last spring, Ls³PrNg
Last summer, Ls³M*R*
Last time, Ls³M
Length of time, Ng³Vm·
Less than, Lsn
Let us be sure, LtsBShr
Long before the time, Ng¹BtM
Long enough, Ng¹Nf
Longer than, Ngrn¹
Lower and lower, LRLR
Make their way, MKtr³W
Makes their, MKstr
May also be, MLSB
May as well have been, MsLvn
May be certain, M³BsRt
May it not have been, Mt³NtBn
May sometimes, MsMms
May therefore, Mtr³F
Mean to be, MnB
Might have been, MtBn
Might not have been, MtNtBn
Monday forenoon, MNDfNn
Month or two, Tbrt
More or less than, MrLsn
More than anybody else, Mrn³NBdLs
Most of the time, MsM
Much more, Ch³M
Must also, MsLS
Must have been, Mstn
Must have known, MsNn
Must not say that, Ms³NtsDh
Must not tell, Ms³NtL
National bank, Ns³Bn
Necessary consequence, NssKns
Need not say anything, Nd¹NusNNg

*Use the loop word-sign for *Is there.*

Next conversation, Ns²Vssn
No connection, NKnsn
No, sir, it is not, NsRtsNt
Nobody else, N²BdLs
Not less than, NtLsn
Not to my knowledge, Nt¹-MNJ
Not to my recollection, Nt¹-MRsn
Nothing else, Ng²Ls
Nothing less, Ng²Ls
Now and then, N²Dhn
Nowhere else, N²RLs
Objected to, as immaterial, Js¹M
Obj. to, as incompetent, Js¹K
Obj. to, as imm. and incom., Js¹MK
Obj. to ; overruled ; exception,
                [J¹VrRldsPsn
Obj. to ; sustained ; exception,
Of course it is, V¹Krsts [J¹ssTtsPsn
Of course there is, V¹Krstrs
Of his own, Vsn¹
Of interest, Vnt¹
Of my own, Vmn¹
Of the sidewalk, Vt¹sDK
Of your own knowledge, Vyn¹NJ
Of yourself, Vy¹sLf
Off and on, Fnr¹
On account (of) rKnt¹
On any other account, rNjKnt¹
On one occasion, chWnKsn
On that date, rDh²Dt
On the contrary, chTrR
On the other side of it, rDhtrsDft
Once or twice, WsTs
One thing and another, WnNgNtr
Or otherwise, Rtr¹Ws [Rd¹NrsTnss
Ordinary circumstances,
Ought not to be, Tn¹B
Ought to be able to, Tt¹BBlt
Ought to have been, Tv¹Bn
Out of the office, Tvt³Fs
Over and above, Vr¹V
Part of the account, Pft²Knt
Peculiar circumstances, PKsTnss
Per annum, PRNm
Per cent., PRsNt
Perhaps they did, PrPsDhd
Piece of land, Ps¹Lnd
Place of residence, PlsRsDns
Plaintiff and defendant, Plnt¹D
Point of view, Pnt¹V
Post mortem examination, PsMsMsn
Post office, PsFs   [PrnNsVd
Preponderance of evidence,
Present time, PrsM
Previous to that time, PrVsDhm
Put an end, Pn³Nd
Question of fact, Kw²Ft
Question of law, KwL
Quite as much, KtsCh⁸
Right angle, Rt¹Gl
Right of way, Rt¹Vw

Sabbath school, sB⁸sKl
Says he did, SsHd
Second time, sKndM
Seems likely, sMs¹LKl
Seems to have been, SmsBn
Several times, sVms
Shall become, ShBK
Shall have been, Shvn
Shall we be, ShwB
She did so, Shd¹S
She never did, Sh¹NVd
She said it was, Sh¹sDtZ
Short time, Shrt¹M
Should not have been, Sh⁸NtBn
Should say so, Shs⁸S
Should you say it was not, Shy⁸StZn
Side by side, sD¹sD
Sign their names, sNtrNms¹
Since his death, sNss¹DTh
Since the other, sNs¹Dhtr
Since they have been, sNsDhvn
Sister in law, Sstrn¹L
So as to be, SsB
So as to have been, SsBn
So far as, SFs
So you may as well, SyMsL
Somebody else, sM²BdLs
Some of the time, sMM
Some other time, sMtrM
Some time or other, sMmRtr
Something has bn said, sMNgs²BnsD
State the conversation, stTtVrssn
State whether it is or not, stWtsRn
State whether or not, stWRn
State whether there is or not,
                [stWtrsRn
Standing there, sTndNgtr
Subject matter, sBMtr
Such an understanding,
           [sChnNdsTndNg
Such as are not, sChsRn
Such as were not, sChsRn
Sunday afternoon, sNDftrNn*
Sure to be, Shrt³B
Take the opportunity, TtPrt
That did it, Dhdch⁸
That is their own, Dhstrn⁸
That such is the fact, Dh³sChstFt
That there has been, Dhtrsn⁸
That we were, Dhww³
That you told us, Dhy⁸Tlds
The next conversation, rNs²Vssn
The other side of it, DhtrsDft
The others, Dhtrs
Their own, Rn
Then there is, Dhntrs   [RsNtChMn
There is not much more than,
There they were, RDhw
There will be, RlB
There will have been, RlBn
They have stated, Dhvst

They have nothing, DhvNg
They say they did, DhsDhd
Think it has been, Ngtsn[1]
Think there has been, Ngtrsn[1]
This cannot be, DhsKnB
This connection, DhsKnsn
Those are not, Dhs[9]Rn
Those that were, Dhs[3]Dhw
Though it had not been, DhtDnBn
Though it were, Dhtw
Though there were, Dhtrw
Though we were, Dhww
Three or four times, ThrFrMs
Thursday evening, ThrsDv
Thus far, ThsF
Time and again, MnGn[1]
To have been, Tv[3]Bn
To make known, Tm[3]Nn
To my knowledge, Tm[3]NJ
To the present time, Tt[3]PrsM
Too far, b[2]F
Too much, b[2]Ch
Toward us, Trds
Tuesday night, TsDn
Under side of it, Nd[2]sDvt
Under the circumstances of the case, United States, Yss[3] [Nd[2]sTnssKs
Unless there is, Nlstrs
Until they are, NtLtr
Up and down, PnDn
Up stairs, Pstrs
Up to that time, PtDhm
Up to the time, PtM
Upon her own account, Prn[1]Knt
Upon his own, Psn[1]
Upon the subject of, Pt[1]sBv
Upon your own, Pyn[1]
Valuable consideration, Vl[3]sDsn
Verdict for the defendant, VrdD
Verdict for the plaintiff, VrdPlnt
Very certain of it, VrsRtVt
Very great extent, VrgrtsTnt
Very little more than, VrLtMrn
Very soon after that time,
Was as good, ZsGd [VrsNFDhm
Was he ever, ZrV
Was he not, ZrNt
Wasn't he, Znch
Ways and means, WsMns
We changed, wCh
We decline, wDKln
We may not have been, W[1]MnBn
We might not be, W[1]MtNtB
We went there, W[1]Wntj
Wednesday morning, WnsDM
Week or two, Krt[1]
Well known, LNn
Were you certain of it, RysRtVt
Were you not informed, RynNF
West line, WsLn
What did you mean, Tdy[1]Mn
What do you mean, T[1]DyMn

What of that, Tv[1]Dh
What is his business, Tss[1]Bss
What is your business, Ts[1]Yss
What time in the month, Tm[1]NtTh
What time in the night, Tm[1]NtNt
What time of day, Tm[1]D
What time of night, Tm[1]Nt
What was the occasion, T[1]ZtKsn
When did you come, HdyK
When do you say, H[2]Dys
When it has been, Htsn
Where are they, RRDh
Where did you go, RdyG
Where there has been, Rtrsn
Where were you going, RtryG
Whether he did or not, WHdRn
Whether he ever did, WrVd
Whether it is or not, WtsRn
Whether it has been, Wtsn
Which did you mean, ChtyMn
Which have been, ChvBn
Which is their own, Chstrn
Which it might, ChtMt
Which would seem, ChwsM
Which year was it, ChyZt
Which you may not remember,
Who came there, jKtr [ChyMnB
Who are they, j[2]RDh
Whoever have, jv[2]V
Who has been, js[2]Bn
Who has not been, jsNt[2]Bn
Who may not have been, jMn[2]Bn
Who were away, jr[2]W
Who were not, j[2]ltn
Who would not have been, j[2]WnBn
Whose was it, Z[2]Zt
Why are we, W[1]Rw
Why did he ever have, Wdr[1]Vv
Why did she, Wd[1]Sh
Why there has been, Wtrsn[1]
Why he did not, W[1]HdNt
Why he ever did it, Wr[1]Vdch
Will be certain, LBsRt
Will have been, Lvn
Will they ever, LDhv
With all its, Dhlts[1]
With himself, Dhms[1]
With interest, Dhnt[1]
With its own, Dhtsn[1]
With which it is not, Dh[1]ChtsNt
Within their own knowledge,
Without interest, Wnt[1] [Dhntr[1]NNJ
Worth having, Thvn
Would be sufficient, w[2]BsFsNt
Year and a half, Yn[1]F
Yes, it is, Ysts
You and he, Ynch[3]
You are acquainted (with), Y[2]Kwnt
You have seen, Yv[3]sN
You have stated, Yvst[3]
You must remember, yMs[2]Br
You say you have been, Ys[3]Yvn

READING EXERCISES.

EARLY REPORTERS.

Webster's Reply to Hayne.

[shorthand notation]

Reporting from Memory.

[shorthand notation]

A Doctored Speech.

[shorthand notation]

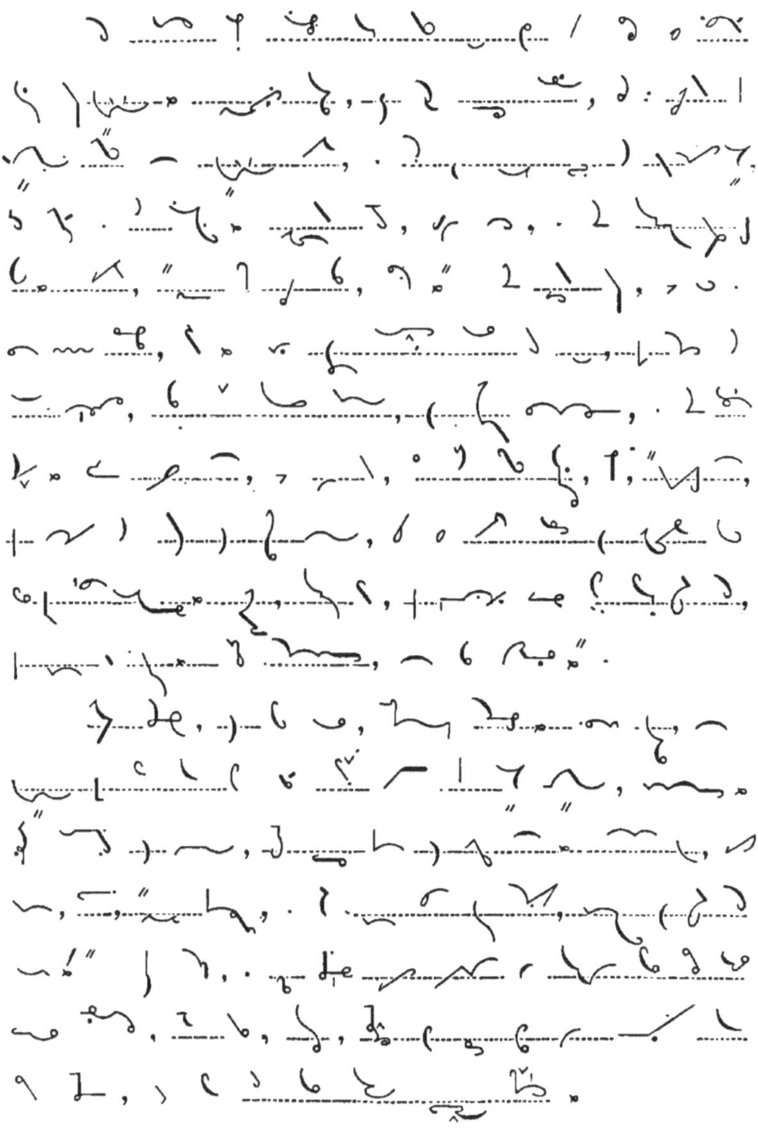

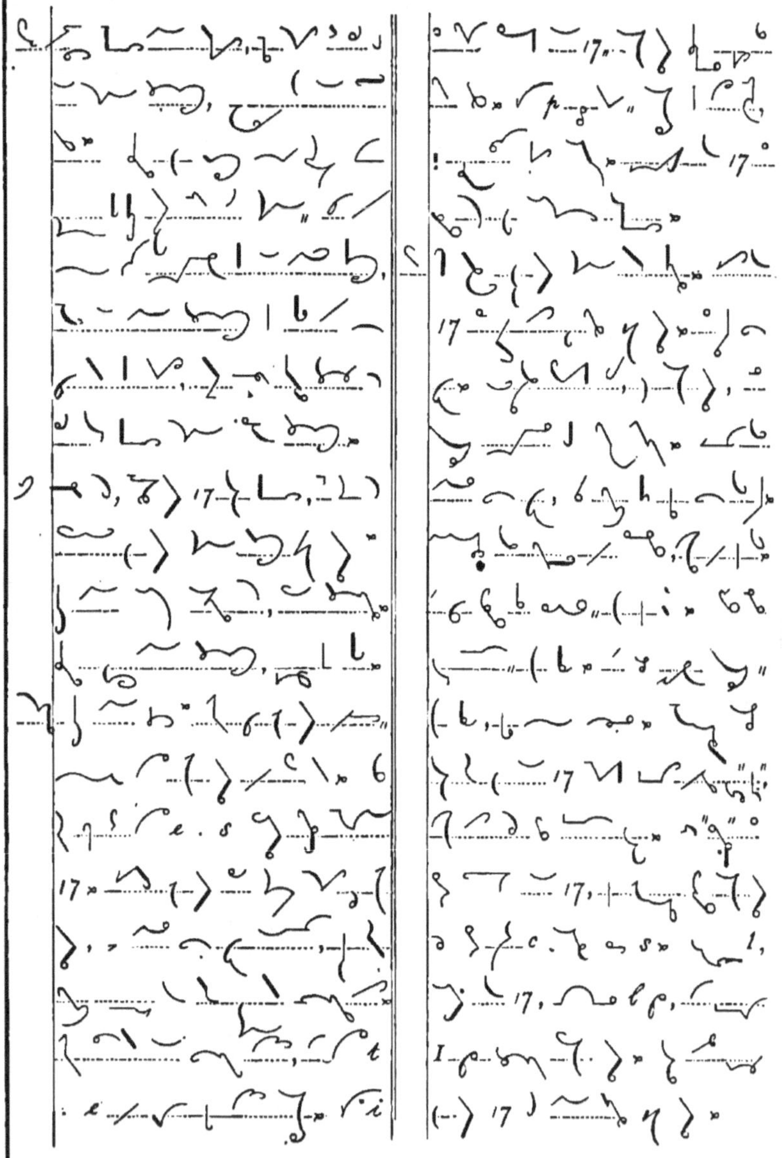

CHARGE TO A JURY.

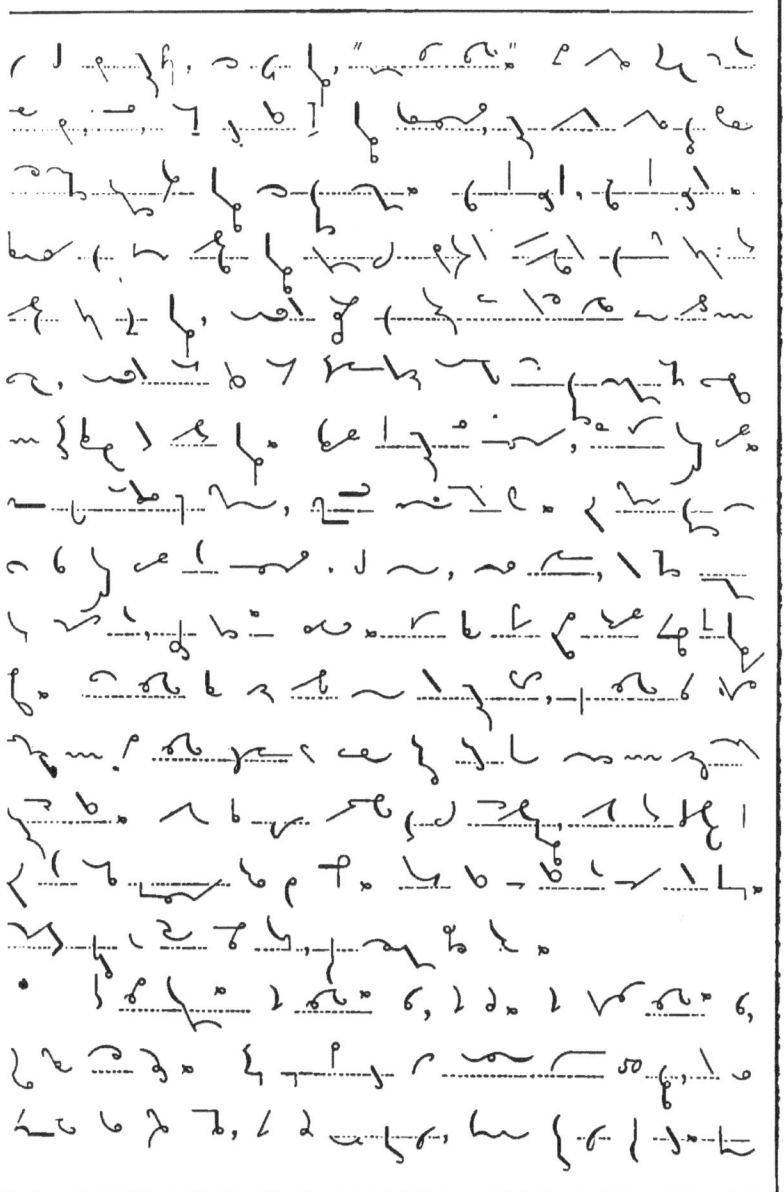

$1059.29

WRITING EXERCISES.

STENOGRAPHERS IN NEW YORK.*

There are many *hundred stenographers in New York* city, *and the number is yearly* increasing. *Most of them* find employment *as* private secretaries *and in* offices *and business houses, at* salaries ranging *from* twelve *to* fifteen *dollars a week* ; *or as* reporters *of* law cases tried *before the* numerous referees, *at a compensation of from* ten *to* fifteen cents *a* folio *of one hundred words. Occasionally, an* expert *is* hired *at a* stated salary *by* some litigant *who does not care to* depend *upon the* official *stenographer for* transcripts *of the* proceedings *in* trials *of his* cases. *During the well-*known trial *of* Sharp, *the defendant* employed *two stenographers for* forty days, *whom he* paid *at the* rate *of* five *dollars an hour.*

Official *stenographers in the New York* courts *are* paid *a* salary *of* $2,500 *a year, with additional* fees *for* transcripts *of their* notes, making *about* $5,000 *a year—and they* earn *it. The work is very* severe, *in long* trials, *for the* record *of a* day's proceedings *must be* written *out before the* opening *of the* court *on the* following day. *As* soon *as the* court *adjourns, the stenographer* hastens *to his* office *with his* notes. *Of course, it would be impossible for him to* transcribe *them himself, within the time* required, *but if he* writes *a* legible *hand he can* turn *over his original* notes *to several* trained copyists, *who* make short *work of it while he* seeks *the* rest *he so much* needs *to prepare him for the next day's* work. *Few of the* older *stenographers are able to do this, however, on account of careless* habits *of writing* induced *by the* defective *systems of* shorthand *they* employ *and which they* learned *long before the* present *improved and* logical *systems were published.* Such *stenographers are compelled to* dictate portions *of their* notes *to several other stenographers, who in* turn dictate *their own* notes *to* rapid *typewriters, the* official *stenographer* dictating *the last* portion *of his* notes *to another typewriter ; and the* click *of the* machines *and the* weary monotone *of the stenographers'* voices *may be* heard far into *the* night. *Men can* stand *a few weeks of such work at a* time, *but it is* sure *to* wear *them out at last.*

Some *of the New York lawyers are very* rapid *speakers, and the best stenographers are* taxed *to their* utmost *to* report *them. It is* said *that*

*Words-signs and contractions are printed in Italic.

many average nearly *two hundred words* a minute. *To* report *such speakers for any length of time, becomes a question of* endurance, *and* many *of the best stenographers have not the* physical *strength to do it.*

It is not strange *that mistakes should occasionally be made by stenographers*—indeed, *it would be* strange *if they were not. They generally occur from* misunderstanding *the words of a* speaker, *or from* misreading *the* notes *in the* hurry *of* transcription. *The* latter *is* most likely *to* cause *such mistakes, especially where it is* necessary *to* dictate *the* notes *to other stenographers. Probably, the most dangerous mistakes are occasioned from* writing *the same* outline *for two or more words which the* context *will not* aid *in distinguishing.* Some *systems of* shorthand *furnish many opportunities for* such *mistakes, as where the words at all and until are* written alike. *If a witness should testify, for* instance, *"I was not in* Brooklyn UNTIL *the first of* March," *the* most expert reporter *or* copyist *from such a system might* readily fall into *the* error *of* writing, *"I was not in* Brooklyn AT ALL, *the first of* March." *The* result *to the witness might be by no* means pleasant, *if he should be* indicted *for* perjury *for* making *the* statement thus attributed *to him.*

Closely associated *with the stenographers in their work is a* vast army *of typewriters, most of them* ladies *of* education *and* culture. *They have their* offices, make *very good* incomes, *and live well. They have a uniform* scale *of* prices, *charging* five cents a folio *for a single* copy, eight cents *for two copies, and* ten cents *for* three. *Some of them become very* expert *in the* use *of the typewriter, and often* write *at the* rate *of* seventy-five *words* a minute, *but of course* such *a* speed *cannot be* kept *up for any great length of time.* Many *of these* ladies *are* experts *in* shorthand, *and are able to take* dictation *from* official *stenographers, and* even *to occupy responsible positions as* reporters. *They are able to* earn *a good* income, *frequently as high as from* $1500 *to* $2500 *a year. Their work,* like *that of* official *stenographers, is often* tedious, *but it is generally very* pleasant *and satisfactory.*

THE USE OF SIMPLE WORDS.

Through life, we all teach and we all learn. This-world is-a great school, where we-find what-is-good and-what-is-bad, and-thus are made-ready *to* act in-another-sphere. What-we-are at-the end of-this life, we-shall-be when-the next[30] begins. We-must-therefore spare no-pains when we-teach others or ourselves. We-teach our-selves in-our thoughts, others by-our words or acts. We-must take care *to* think and-speak in-a-way so-clear that·we do-not-cheat or mislead ourselves by vague and-hazy[100] ideas. We·must learn *to* think in words, and we-must get a-habit of-using them in thought with-the-same care with-which we-speak or write *to* others. Words give-a body and-form to-our thoughts, without which they-are apt *to* be so-dreamy and-unreal[150] that-we do-not-see where they-are weak or-false. If-we put-them into-words, we-shall learn how-much-of truth there-is-in-them. When in-that form, we-can turn them over in-our-minds. If-we write-them out, we-find that in-many-cases[200] the ideas we-thought-we-had hold of fade-away under-the test. If-they-do prove *to* be of-real value, they-are thus not-only made clear to-us but-they-are in-such-shape that-we may-make-them clear *to* others. When ideas float[250] in-our-minds and we-are in-doubt about-them, our doubts may often be-solved by talking with-others, for if-, we state-them clearly we-see-the-truth at-once. It-is what-we-say *to* others, in-most cases, that settles our doubts, not what-they-say to-us.[300]

We-must not-only think in words, but-we-must-also try *to* use-the best words, words which-will most clearly put into-the-minds of others the ideas which-are resting in-our-own minds. This-is-the great art *to* be-gained by-those-who wish *to*[350] teach in-the-school, in-the-church, at-the-bar, or through-the-press. To-do-this in-the right-way, they should as-a-rule use-the short words which-we learn in-early-life, and-which-have-the same-sense to-all-classes of-men. Those-are-the-best[400] for-the-teacher, the-orator, and-the poet.

Look at-what-has-been said in prose or in-verse that-has come-down to-us through-many-years, and-you-will-find that-it-is in short words. Count them in Gray's Elegy, and-you-will-find that a-large-share[450] of-the-words are of-this-class. The-English of-the-Bible is-good, but now-and-then some long words are-found, and-they always hurt-the verse in-which-you-find them. Take-that which says, "O generation-of-vipers, who hath warned-you *to* flee from-the-wrath[500] *to* come ?" There-is one word which ought-not-to-have-been used—*generation*. In-the-older version the-word *brood* is-used. When-the verse is read with-that word in-place of-the-other, its full force is-felt.

In-your thoughts and in-your speech use[550] short, plain terms, and-you-will-find your meaning will-be much clearer to-yourself and-to-others.[568]

NOTE.—The above exercise is an excellent one for dictation practice, as it contains the simplest words only. The student should not be satisfied that he has received all the benefit to be gained from it until he is able to write it from dictation in *four minutes.*

Words to be joined in phrasing, are connected by hyphens. When *to* is to be indicated by proximity, it is printed in Italic.

A TYPEWRITER FORGERY.

Q.—If-you-were required *to* examine a-document written by-the-typewriter, and-to-say whether-or-not all-the sheets contained in-it were-written upon-the-same-machine, could-you-answer with any degree-of positiveness ? **A.**—It-is-possible that two-machines may-write so-nearly alike as-to-make-it difficult *to* determine upon-which-of-them a-particular sheet was-written ; still there-are many little marks-of difference in-the writing-of different-machines, and-even in-the writing of-the-same-machine at different-times or when used by different operators, by-which-an expert ought-to-be-able-to-say with-some-certainty whether-the sheets of-a document were-written consecutively upon-the-same-machine.

Q.—I-show-you exhibit one, and-call-your-attention *to* page 17 of-that document, and-I ask whether in-your-opinion that page was-written by-the-machine which-wrote-the-other pages ? **A.**—It-was-not written in-the-order in-which-it-appears here, nor by-the-same-person. It-is-possible that-it-may-have-been written by-the-same-machine, but-it-must-have-been at-a different-time.

Q.—Why-do-you-say it-was-not written at-the-same-time ? **A.**—The-type used on-that page are-clean ; many-of-the letters on-the-other pages are filled up. This-is especially true with-regard-to-the letters *e* and *s* in-all-the-pages preceding and-following 17. The-ribbon on-that page is-not so-much worn as-it-is on-the-other pages, and-the writing-is more uniform in-color, but-that is-to-be partially accounted for by-the-fact that-it-was-written by a-more-practiced writer. The-type seem *to* be in more-perfect alignment, while-the letters *t* and *e* are badly out-of alignment in-the-other-sheets. The-letter *i* is properly centered in 17 ; in-the-other pages it-strikes to-the-left of-its proper position. The-letter *p* stands upright ; in-the-other-sheets it leans a-trifle, owing to-its-being slightly turned in-the-bar. The-margin of 17 is two-spaces wider than in-the-remainder of-the-document.

Q.—Upon-what do-you base-your-opinion that-that page was-written by-a different-person ? **A.**—The-writer of 17 is-a much-better writer than-the person who-wrote-the-other pages. His touch-is more uniform. None of-his-letters over-ride each-other, as in-the-other pages, and-his punctuation marks do-not perforate the-paper. The-color of-his writing-is more uniform, which-is partially due to-his more-even touch. The-indentations of-his paragraphs are six-spaces, while-the-others are but five. He uses three-spaces between-his sentences ; the-other but two. He-places a-space after-a comma ; the-other does-not. He understands the-rules-of-punctuation ; the-other does-not, but-makes many mistakes. A-very-noticeable instance of-that is-the-fact that in 17 a-period and-colon are-placed after-the-words ·"*to-wit.*," while-the-other writer always places a-comma after-them. The-word "*supersede*" is spelled correctly in 17, but I-have-noticed three-places in-the-other pages where-it-is spelled with-the-letter *c* in-place-of-the second *s*. For-the-figure 1, in-the-paging of 17, a-lower-case *l* is-used, while a-capital *I* is-used for-the-same-purpose in-all-the-other pages. For-these reasons, I-am-certain that page 17 was-not written by-the-person who-wrote-the-other pages.

CHARGE TO A JURY. ·

Gentlemen-of-the-Jury: In-the-case about *to* be submitted to-you, you-have a-duty *to* perform which-is-as-important as-that-of the-Court. The-duties of-the-jury and-of-the-Court are distinctly separated. It-is-the duty of-the-Court *to* instruct-you upon-all-questions-of-law, and-first of-all, as-to-what questions-of-fact you-are *to* decide, and-it-is-your duty *to* find only upon-such questions-of-fact as-shall-be submitted to-you by-the-Court.

In-this-case, there-is-but a single-question-of-fact for-your-consideration, and-that-is-the question of-the good-faith of-the-transaction by-which Palmer received-the-draft in-question from-the defendants. Several-questions-of-fact have-been alluded to by-counsel 'in-your-presence. which-you-will-not-be called upon *to* decide, the-Court holding that-they-are not-involved in-this-action.

The-question whether Palmer was-the owner of-this draft, depends upon-the-question whether, in-receiving-it from-the defendants, he-exercised towards-them that good-faith which as-their banker he-was-bound *to* exercise, or-whether-his conduct in-receiving-it was-a-violation of-that good-faith. The-question whether-the City Bank was-a holder of-this draft for-value, is-not in-the-case. Whatever was-sent by-that bank *to* Palmer, was-sent without any-anticipation of-this draft, and without any-knowledge that-such a-draft was in-existence or-ever would-be, or-whether it-would-ever-be offered *to* them. I-instruct-you, therefore, that-the City Bank was-not a-holder of-the-draft for-value.

I-further instruct-you that-the-plaintiffs in-this-case were-not holders-of-the-draft for-value. The-law in-regard-to-the title *to* commercial paper is well settled and-well understood. A-person who takes commercial paper before by-its-terms it becomes-due, without notice of-any-defense existing against-it, paying value for-it at-the-time-he takes-it, holds-it discharged of-all-defenses which-can-be set up against-it by-the-maker of-the-paper. These three things are-necessary, however, in-order-that-the holder of-such paper shall thus hold-it independent of-defenses: That-he shall take-it in-good-faith; that-he shall take-it for-value—for-a consideration parted with for-it; and-that-he shall thus take-it before-it becomes-due. In-this-case, there-was-no parting with-value for-the paper [p. 104], and-no pretense of-it, or, at-least, but-a mere-pretense. When-the-cashier of-the-bank said to-the agent of-the-plaintiffs, "Here-are papers to-the-amount of-your-deposits, and here-is-a-check for-you *to* sign for-your-balance," did-the-plaintiffs pay anything for-the securities that-were at-that-time delivered *to* them? Not-a-dollar. He-was-asked *to* give-his-check, and-he gave-it *to* stand over against-this payment ; but-the turning out of-those securities was, in-point-of-fact and-in-point-of-law, a-mere payment of-a liability which previously existed on-the part-of-the-bank to-the-plaintiffs—and-the turning out of-commercial paper in-payment of-a preëxisting liability is-not a-transfer for-value. Such-is-the law. It does-not pay-it, and-unless-the transfer prove *to* be-good, the-creditor still has-his claim upon-the-original indebtedness. Suppose a-man comes to-you with a-note of-a hundred-dollars, apparently good, and-offers-it to-you in-payment of-a debt, and-you accept-it—unless-that note is-collectible, it does-not pay-the-claim, and-you still have-the-right *to* proceed against-the-debtor upon-the-original demand. It-is given to-you in-payment of-that existing indebtedness, and-you take-it only upon condition that-it-is good and-collectible. When-you-seek *to* enforce-it, if-the-maker have-a perfect-defense against-it in-the-hands of-your-debtor, he-has that perfect-defense against-it in-your-hands. There must-be a-parting with-value for commercial paper, in-order-that-there may-be a-holding discharged-of defenses which otherwise would-exist to-the paper. So, I-charge-you, as-matter-of-law, that-the-plaintiffs were-not holders for-value.

This, you-see, brings-us to-the single-question-of-fact whether Palmer acted in-good-faith with-his customers the-defendants, or in-bad-faith and-fraudulently, when-he received-this paper. If-he-did-act in-bad-faith and-fraudulently, that-fraud rendered-his holding of-it invalid, and-no-man could thereafter hold-it in-good-faith unless-he paid value, which neither-the City Bank nor-the-plaintiffs did.

Come-then to-the-question whether Palmer took-this paper in-good-faith or-fraudulently. When a-person proclaims-himself to-the world as-a banker, ready *to* receive-the-deposits of-his customers, he thereby holds-himself out as-a-man of-sufficient means *to* meet-the obligations he thus assumes. Whether-his-responsibilty is-large or small, is of-no-consequence ; he-represents-himself *to* be a-man of-means large-enough *to* meet these obligations [105]. You do-not expect a-banker *to* state-to-you, whenever you-make-a deposit, "I-am still solvent." Such-a representation was-never heard of, and-is-not expected, because, in-doing-a banking business and-taking-the deposits of-his customers, a-banker thereby represents that-he-has sufficient means *to* meet-a-demand for-the-payment of-such deposits whenever that-demand may-be-made. That-is what he-is-bound *to* do, and-that-is what he-is-bound *to* be. It-is-not-necessary that, at-the-time-he received-these deposits, Palmer should-have expected *to* fail *to* pay or *to* refuse *to* pay that particular paper; if-he received-that paper as-a deposit, knowing himself *to* be in-such-circumstances that if-he-were called upon *to* meet-his liabilities he-could-not respond—moreover, knowing-himself *to* be in-a position in-which he-was-likely *to* be-rendered incapable-of meeting that-demand when-it-should-be-made in-the-due course-of-business—he-was-bound *to* dis-close-that-fact before-he received-the deposit. This-relation between a-banker and-his customer, is-a highly confidential relation. You-go to-him not *to* buy-his-goods and-to pay-your-money, but-you-go *to* give-him your-money *to* keep for-you. Shall-it-be permitted that-a-man may hold this confidential relation with customers and take-their-money when-he-is likely, before a-demand can-be-made for-a return of-it, to-suspend payment? Certainly-not. The-law does-not tolerate such-an-abuse of-the-relation which-exists between-a depositary and-his-depositor. Mere insolvency does-not render-the receipt-of money by a-banker fraudulent, but insolvency which-is hopeless and-irremediable, such insolvency as-is-likely *to* compel-the closing of-the-doors of-the-bank at-any moment, renders-it improper for-the-banker *to* continue-the business. Therefore it-is that-the-law requires-of-him that-he shall-not continue *to* receive-deposits, or-that, if-he does-receive-them, it shall-be with notice to-the-customer of-the-facts as-they exist. Upon-no-other basis could-the business of-the country be conducted. We-are-obliged to-have-banks for-the ordinary exchanges of-trade, but-they must-not-be-made instruments of-fraud.

What-was-the situation of-Palmer? Was-he insolvent? Yes, so-he says. Was-he hopelessly insolvent? Yes, so-far-as present means were-concerned. He-was-indebted to-the City Bank alone in-something like 50 thousand-dollars, upon notes which-he-had-given to-a friend for-his personal accommodation, which-he says-he knew had-been used, though-he-did-not-know they-had-been used at-that bank. But-he-did-know [106] that-they-were outstanding obligations against-him. To-his-customers, he owed over 50 thousand-dollars for deposits received by-him. The-amount of-his assets was very inconsiderable, compared with-this large liability. That-he-was hopelessly insolvent, you-will-probably be compelled *to* find. Now, what-was-his ground of expectation? He-says-he-had-an arrangement with-the City Bank *to* furnish-him money as-he wanted-it.

That arrangement must-have-had two-sides, we-should-suppose, and so we-find-the-fact *to* be, for-he-was *to* furnish-the City Bank with paper equal in amount to-the-currency furnished to-him. But-it-was-not so-much upon-that that-he relied as upon-the expectation that-his-friend, who-was-the president of-the City Bank, should "carry him." I-charge-you, as-matter-of law, that-a-man cannot honestly carry on the-business of-banking upon a-mere-promise of-another *to* carry-him, without-some security for-the-performance of-the-promise. It-cannot-be tolerated that-a-man shall continue such-a-business upon-the mere assurance of-another, without-security, that-he will carry-him. Whenever that other ceases *to* carry-him, there-is-an-end-of-it, and-the depositors go without-their-money. A-man cannot do-a banking business honestly without means or reasonable expectation of-means *to* do-the-business with. That-is so-simple a-proposition that-it-seems unnecessary *to* state-it. What-is common-sense in-a-case of-this-kind, is-the-law of-the-case, and-the law must commend-itself to-the-good-judgment of-the-jury.

As I-have-stated, the-only-question-of-fact upon-which-you-are-to-find, is-whether this-deposit was-received by Palmer in-good-faith, or-whether, under-the-circumstances-of-the-case, it-was dishonest on-his-part *to* receive-it. I-repeat, that-it-is-not-necessary that-there should-have-been an-intention in-this particular-case *to* defraud the-men who-made-the deposit ; if-a-man is-doing-a banking-business fraudulently all-the-time, it-is-not-necessary that-he shall entertain a-particular fraudulent design in-each individual case in-which-he receives-deposits. If-this transaction was-thus fraudulent on-the part-of Palmer, the-defense is-established, because-he thereby obtained no-title to-the-draft in-question, and-the City Bank obtained no-title unless he-did. If-you-find that-this was-an-honest transaction, the-plaintiffs are-entitled-to-your verdict for-the-amount of-the-draft, which-is $1,059.29. If-it-was-not an-honest transaction, your-verdict must-be for-the-defendants.

Mr. Gillette asked-the court *to* charge-the-jury that-it-was necessary for-the-defendants *to* establish-the-fact that Palmer misrepresented the-facts with-the intention of-deceiving them, and-that-he obtained the-draft by-means of-such-misrepresentations.

Refused ; exception.

Also, that-the answer could-not-be-sustained unless-the defendants were in-fact deceived.

Refused ; exception.

Mr. Gillette excepted to-the charge that-the City Bank was-not a-holder for-value.

Also, to-the charge that-the-plaintiffs were-not holders for-value.

Verdict for-the-defendants.

CONTRACTIONS AND WORD-FORMS.*

1. Dear *Sir :*—We shall not be able-to complete the *purchase* of the *Hoadley* property at *present.* The messenger we *sent* was notified by some-one in the neighborhood that the *estate* was heavily mortgaged, and upon *further* inquiry it was learned that the chattel-mortgage was *overdue ;* and inasmuch as the fact was afterwards *disclosed* that the obligation secured by the real-estate bond-and-mortgage would mature in November, the negotiation in-relation-to the transfer was discontinued, under the advice of the lawyer who *acted* as counsel for the administrator, and with his approval.

If circumstances shall at any time *warrant* a *renewal* of the negotiation, we will notify you at-once.

2. My Dear *Sir :*—Your letter of inquiry as to the *political standing* of Mr. *Perkins* can be *answered* in a few *words.* He is very changeable. He was formerly a distinguished representative of Democracy ; next, a dignified Republican legislator ; then, an Independent, characterized by the most positive opinions ; and he now undertakes to demonstrate the truth of his original convictions as a Democrat, in acknowledgement of a conditional *promise* of a nomination by the party to a position of importance for which I understand he has long negotiated, in the expectation that everything connected with his former inconsideration will be forgotten or forgiven by intelligent *voters.*

If the committee *desire* more particular information, it will be *promptly* furnished.

3. Gentlemen :—I have referred your communication of the *20th instant* to Mr. *Bacon.* His *reply* was *dictated* by him to his stenographer, and he wishes me to *repeat* it to you. It is in these *words :*

"The perpendicular portion naturally became particularly important, in an architectural and mechanical *sense,* for the proper and efficient *support* and maintenance of the easterly extension of the principal building of the university, notwithstanding its intersection with the northeastern *structure ;* nevertheless, the inexperience and *lack* of comprehension of the superintendent, who had undertaken

---

*In these exercises, all the principles of phrasing are to be used. The outlines for the words printed in Italic are to be supplied by the student. The proper outlines for all the other words are contained in the table of Word-Signs and the alphabetical lists of Contractions and Word-Forms heretofore given. Words connected by hyphens are to be written with a single outline.

independently to certify to its sufficiency, so characteristic of his *want* of intelligence, should have *led* the *trustees* to anticipate the imperfect workmanship, and the consequent occurrence of an accident of that description, involving the authorities of the institution in the expense and danger of an *action* for negligence."

If I can be of *further assistance* to you in the *matter, please* inform me.

4. Dear *Carrie :*—In my *last letter* I spoke of our *drive* on *Grand Avenue.* We *found* a good-deal of wealth represented in the architecture of that portion of the *city,* equaling anything we have any remembrance of having before discovered in our *journey.* This was *noticeable* in our first superficial observation of the buildings, but the *constant succession* of *elegant structures* was very remarkable. It is difficult to describe the effect upon us of this *wonderful exhibition.* In fact, no description could possibly represent it. It is beyond my *ability* to relate, or yours to imagine, the many objects of interest which we were given an opportunity to examine, and which we observed on-either-hand as we continued our *course* among these *countless* attractions. It was afterwards our privilege to *visit* and examine the internal arrangements of *some* of the dwellings, and we *found* them quite equal to what we had been *led* to expect from their external appearance. Although entire strangers, we were *received* with *hearty* welcome, and every *effort* was made to *render* our *visit* a pleasure to us, and it was certainly very *pleasant.* We could *scarcely* suppress a *constant* expression of surprise at the uniform *elegance* and *taste exhibited* in the manner in which the houses were *arranged,* and in the character and *beauty* of their furniture.

The buildings *erected* by the various religious denominations were especially worthy of attention. They showed at-once a *healthy* financial condition, and the *capability* of their architects and mechanics, and to our delighted view they appeared the *height* of perfection. There was nothing about them that we could-not fully approve.

As we *reached* the Catholic *cathedral,* we saw a large *crowd* about the *entrance.* We inquired the occasion, and were informed that the day was an anniversary observed by Roman Catholics throughout the world. As the *services* had commenced, we did not go in, but we shall try to *visit* it *tomorrow.* The building itself is magnificent, and in its *interior* it is said to *surpass* any similar *edifice* in *Europe.* I shall give you a description of it in my next. For *today,* this *short letter,* and the *photographs* accompanying it, must *suffice.*

5. Dear *Sir :*—We have *just* come from a *meeting* of the repre-sentatives of the operatives, and we now give you a *brief statement* of the *result.* The conversation was somewhat disconnected, at first, and for a good-while few who spoke acknowledged in any-way the natural signification or the probable consequences of *·such* a con-troversy, or the disadvantage and practical disorganization which we claimed must immediately *result* from this opposition. They were averse to any movement to establish the projected reform, declaring that *unless* it was mutually agreed upon, and voluntary, it would *excite* a revolution. This assumption we *denied.* We had special satisfaction in the speech of one of the men, who appeared to be perfectly familiar with the situation. A significant remark of his was, that the continual *trouble* we have had was occasioned largely by passion, which affected their minds and *prevented* any-other than a superficial view of the case. He acquiesced in the claim that they *gained* strength by combining, but he was apprehen-hensive that instead of preserving their *rights* by the formation of such a combination, they would *soon* become disorganized, or, at-all-events, would altogether *fail* to avert the danger which would otherwise *confront* them. He *said* nobody was more chargeable with originating the *trouble* than themselves, that they were capable of securing the preservation of their *rights* if they would take a more comprehensive view of the facts, and that they might thus *gain* a profit greater-than ever before, and more continuous.

During this speech, he was frequently *interrupted.* Some-of-the-time, he was *contradicted;* sometimes they tried to argue·with him ; but for most-of-the-time his representations were *listened* to in *silence.* No-other than an influential man belonging to themselves could have spoken so well. Before he began, nearly everybody considered it an extravagant measure, and it was difficult to satisfy any-one that the expenditure was indispensibly necessary. It is now understood that the combined *efforts* of those interested will perhaps *result* in a comparision of views and a consideration of the argu-ments *advanced,* and *induce* the greater number of them to accept the suggestion and *assist* in influencing a compliance with so advan-tageous an *offer.* Meantime, several gentlemen are engaged in endeavoring to secure a reformation of the contract between the manufacturers and individual workmen, and it is hoped that the work may *soon* be satisfactorily reorganized. With organization, *capital* and experience, we are sure of *ultimate success.*

6. The learned judge charged the jury that the plaintiff was required to furnish a preponderance of proof, in-order-to maintain his contention—that he must prove, by testimony applicable to the *case* and satisfactory to themselves, every *allegation* constituting the cause-of-action set-forth in his complaint. He remarked that they should not be influenced by sympathy, but should examine circumstantially each *item* testified to, the appearance and manner of each witness, and all the probabilities of the *case*, for the purpose of *reaching* a correct decision in-accordance-with the facts; and that, on-the-other-hand, they *must* arrive at a determination without-regard-to any-other influence, or any *prejudice*, remembering that all men are equal before the law. He referred especially to the hand-writing of the signatures to a number of the memoranda and other instruments in-writing, and gave them careful instruction with-respect-to the situation of the parties. He explained at-length the question at issue, and described what would constitute an actionable *offense* against the plaintiff's rights. He instructed them that a mistake of judgment or a *failure* to comprehend his obligation would disqualify a *juror* for discharging his whole *duty*, which was to deliver a verdict in-accordance-with the truth.

7. The *president* of the Commercial Bank is a very influential gentleman, and he is universally respected. By the last will and testament of his *deceased* brother, he was nominated as executor. The *widow* had expected to be designated as executrix, and she was indignant that her claims had not been *recognized*. Her brother-in-law disclaimed any *desire* for the position, and after the preliminary proofs had been taken he *proposed* to *resign*, and suggested that she be made administratrix. She was *unable* to furnish the *necessary* security, however, and by common *consent* of those interested he continued to act. It had been commonly believed that the *deceased* was very wealthy, but upon a particular examination of his accounts and the completion of the *inventory*, it was discovered that for a year-or two before his *death* he was on the *verge* of bankruptcy, his business *affairs* being so involved that he was really of no pecuniary responsibility whatever. The family being thus *reduced* to poverty, the brother undertook to *supply means* sufficient to make them *comfortable*, and they will, during the next-month, *remove* to a pretty *cottage* which he has had built for them.

8. A peculiar subject of public interest is furnished in the published accounts with-regard-to the new rules issued by the general government in-respect-to transactions between *citizens* of different *states*, and particularly to financial arrangements between domestic *corporations* and mercantile houses which have heretofore been able to *obtain* a discrimination in *prices* for the *transmission* of *freight* over our great railways. Whether an exception will be

made in-respect-of express companies, is a question upon which no certain information has as yet been given. Within a day-or-two, nominations of members of the commission will be sent to the senate.

9. It is impossible to declare any reasonable suggestion why these companies should be excepted from a *regulation* of *such* import. Anything so extraordinary and questionable has heretofore been unknown, as this *supposed* improvement in the administration of this part of the *service*. It is suggestive of direct and improper influence upon the person commissioned to take charge of *postal affairs*, entirely different and dissimilar to those which common people possess or are able-to *exercise* to compel administrative *officers* to discriminate between them and others in the practical operation of a law, when we consider that it will *confer* upon these combinations a privilege so dangerous to the revenue. Why should anybody, engaged in any occupation, be thus punished, in the performance of his usual *avocation*, and the *disposition* of his manufactures or merchandise or exchanges be questioned or challenged, or his compliance with his regular *agreements* be *prevented*, and additional disqualifications be determined upon by inconsiderate *officials*, to disorganize trade and to put difficulties in the way of commercial transactions? If it is decreed that manufactories and banks and business establishments are to be substantially *forced* to assignments by the application of this rule, we apprehend that *loss* of personal security may *follow* the *loss* of property.

10. What is the significance of this unconsidered resolution? What is to be its longer continuation, or the possibility of the frequency and duration of its distinct and unconditional *enforcement?* What justification dignifies the declaration of *such* a discrimination? What doctrine determines its indispensible *necessity*, or requires this commission of injustice? How inconsistent are the extravagant technical arguments in explanation of the determination to compel acquiescence in this transition toward financial destruction! The circumstances connected with this destructive demonstration by the dignified and consequential gentleman who assumes to be the corrector and governor of the *postal affairs* of the republic, and who is really responsible for the bewildering *sense* of insecurity and apprehension so universally *felt*, are *arousing such* indignation and *anger* as should at-least lead him to *heed* the expression of the dissatisfaction so universally *entertained*. The complication is exceedingly *serious*, and we trust that it will at-once attract the attention of the authorities, and that they will *teach* a *lesson* to this transient proficient in legislation that will be instructive to *such* as he for all time to come.

OPTIONAL EXPEDIENTS.

The expedients given below are intended for the use of expert writers only. Students should not attempt to use them, until they have had considerable experience in actual work. Some of the special phrasing contractions are included in the table of Illustrative Phrases, and will be suggestive to the intelligent stenographer.

ATTENTION.—The small circle and back-hook may be used for *attention*, when that word ends a phrase; as in the phrases, *Was your attention*, Zysn[2]; *Called my attention*, Kld[1]Msn.

BUT may be indicated, at the beginning of a clause or a sentence, by the T-tick resting on the line.

FORTH.—The use of the F-hook may be extended, by using it to add *forth*; as, *Call forth*, Klf[1]; *Put forth*, Pf[3].

HUSBAND may be written sBnd, at the end of a phrase.

I.—In law reporting, *I* may be omitted from the phrases *I did not, I do not, I had not*, where such phrase comprises the whole of the answer of a witness.

I may be omitted where it occurs the second time, in such phrases as *I don't know as I did; I don't know as I can; I don't know as I ever did.*

I may be written with the K-tick, in the middle or end of a phrase, where the T-tick cannot be used; as, *May I not*, MkNt.

KT is often expressed by halving a preceding stem; as *Prospect*, Prs[1]Pt; *Inspect*, Ns[1]Pt.

RECOLLECT may sometimes be indicated by Ray struck downward, after an N-hook; as in *I don't recollect.*

REMEMBER may be indicated by B, in a phrase where Br cannot be joined; as, *I don't remember*, rDnB.

REPETITION.—The repetition of a phrase may be noted by $\wp$, written at points where the repetition occurs; as in the sentence / " *You will carefully consider the testimony of each witness......the opportunity he had for observation......his bearing upon the stand......the apparent candor or lack of candor in his manner of testifying......the amount of interest he has in the result of the action,*" etc.

SESSION.—In convention reporting, the large circle and back-hook may add the word *session*; as, *At that session*, T[2]Thssn.

STREET.—The small loop may be used for *street*, where it can be added to the name of a street; as, *Lake street*, LKst.

SEMI-CIRCLES may be used in such phrases as *Those were the*, Dhs[3]wch; *What is your recollection?* Ts[1]yRsn; *Because we were*, Ks[1]ww.

TO may be indicated, at the beginning of a sentence or line, by writing the succeeding word entirely below the line.

TO HAVE.—The use of the F-hook may be extended, to add *to have*; as, *Said to have*, sDf; *Expect to have*, sPf[3].

THINK may be written with Th, in phrases where Ng will not make a distinct angle.

TIME OF DAY.—Attention is called to the manner of indicating the hour, in connection with the name of the day of the week, in the Illustrative Phrases.

WH.—The B-tick may sometimes be used for *wh*, where the J-tick cannot be used. If the former be used before L, the downstroke may be used, even where the word contains no other stem; as, *Whistle*, bsL[1].

YES; YES, SIR.—S[2] and Ss[2]R may be used for these expressions, if preferred. In such a sentence as *Did he say, Yes?* the word should be written Ys[2].

INDEX.